从经典作家进入历史

希尼在贝拉希的泥炭地，一九八六年
（Bobbie Hanvey 摄）

希尼出生于北爱尔兰德里郡。他的第一本诗集《一个博物学家之死》初版于一九六六年，后又出版了诗歌、批评和翻译作品，使他成为他那一代诗人中的翘楚。一九九五年，他获得诺贝尔文学奖；两度荣获惠特布莱德年度图书奖（《酒精水准仪》，1996；《贝奥武甫》，1999）。由丹尼斯·奥德里斯科尔主持的访谈录《踏脚石》出版于二〇〇八年；他的最后一本诗集《人之链》获得二〇一〇年度前瞻诗歌奖最佳诗集奖。二〇一三年，希尼去世。他翻译的维吉尔《埃涅阿斯纪》第六卷在其去世后出版（2016），赢得批评界盛誉。

◇中英双语版◇

斯泰森岛

山楂灯笼

[爱尔兰] 谢默斯·希尼 著　朱玉 译

广西师范大学出版社
· 桂林 ·

斯泰森岛

1984

给布莱恩·弗里尔

目 录

第一部分

011	地下铁	237
012	梳 妆	238
013	黑刺李杜松子酒	239
014	远离那一切	240
016	契诃夫在萨哈林	242
018	砂岩纪念品	243
020	保存期限	244
020	1. 花岗岩碎片	244
021	2. 老熨斗	244
022	3. 旧锡盘	245
023	4. 道 钉	246
024	5. 来自德尔斐的石头	247
025	6. 雪 鞋	247
027	迁 徙	248
031	最后的目光	251
034	回忆马里布	253

036　陌生化　255

038　出生地　256

041　变　易　258

043　阿尔斯特的暮色　259

045　路上的蝙蝠　261

047　给凯瑟琳·安的榛木棍　262

049　给迈克尔和克里斯托弗的风筝　263

051　铁路儿童　264

052　甜　豆　265

053　布伦的幻象　266

054　赤颈鸭　267

055　希拉纳吉　268

058　小　路　270

061　采砂场　272

061　1. 一九四六　272

061　2. 复员的瓦匠　272

063　3. 沙的暴发　273

064　4. 砖石保存了什么　274

065　渠堤之王　275

第二部分：斯泰森岛

073　斯泰森岛　281

第三部分：斯威尼重生

119　　第一条批注　　　　　　　　311

120　　斯威尼重生　　　　　　　　312

121　　松　开　　　　　　　　　　313

122　　在山毛榉中　　　　　　　　314

124　　第一个王国　　　　　　　　315

125　　第一次飞行　　　　　　　　316

127　　飘　游　　　　　　　　　　318

129　　警　觉　　　　　　　　　　319

130　　教　士　　　　　　　　　　320

132　　隐　士　　　　　　　　　　321

133　　大　师　　　　　　　　　　322

135　　抄　工　　　　　　　　　　323

137　　一个清醒的梦　　　　　　　324

138　　在栗树里　　　　　　　　　325

140　　斯威尼的归来　　　　　　　326

141　　冬　青　　　　　　　　　　327

142　　艺术家　　　　　　　　　　328

143　　旧圣像　　　　　　　　　　329

144　　忆往昔　　　　　　　　　　330

145　　在路上　　　　　　　　　　331

第一部分

地下铁

我们在拱形隧道中奔跑，
你穿着蜜月大衣加速向前，
而我，我当时像一个捷足的神
追赶你，在你变成一株芦苇

或某种初放而泛红的白花之前
大衣疯狂摇摆，纽扣一颗颗
弹开并散落一地
落在地下铁与艾伯特厅之间。

度蜜月，月下游，误了漫步音乐会，
我们的回声消失在回廊而如今
我就像汉塞尔沿着月光下的石子
原路折返，捡起那些纽扣

最终来到一处凄风残灯的站台
列车都走了，潮湿的轨道
和我一样暴露而紧张，全神
贯注于你跟随的脚步，回头即诅咒。

梳　妆

白色毛巾浴袍

腰带松着，头发湿着，

胸底的初凉

像掌中的圣餐杯。

我们的身体是圣灵的

庙宇。[①]记得吗？

还有又小又紧的开衩布套

在圣器上规律

穿脱？还有十字褡

被如此熟练地脱下？但还是穿上

你教给我的词语

和我爱的面料吧：双宫绸。

---

① 引自《哥林多前书》6:19。（此类脚注为译者注，下同，不另标出）

黑刺李杜松子酒

杜松的晴朗天气
渐渐暗成冬天。
她把杜松子酒注入黑刺李
然后封上玻璃容器。

当我旋开它
我闻到灌木丛
被惊扰的酸涩宁静
弥漫在食物储藏室。

当我倒出它
它有锋利的刀刃
并燃烧
明亮的参宿四。

我向你敬酒
以氤氲的、蓝黑的、
光洁的刺李，苦涩
且可靠。

远离那一切

一个冷钢叉
刺探鱼缸水
叉起一只龙虾：
有关节的嫩枝，雨花石，
沉没军火的颜色。

海滨尽收眼底，
海风拍打高窗，
我们把龙虾扔进水烫红，
然后就着最后的爪子
秘密座谈数小时。

是暮光，暮光，暮光
许多问题跃起又落地。
是桨手们的背影和船桨
用力划动又扬起。
加把劲儿，我的朋友，

加油喝干酒底，
真诚攻击，

当海面暗了

又白然后又暗去

而旁征博引涌起

仿佛背诵不在现场的证词：

我被牵掣于两极之间，

一边是对静止原点的冥思，

一边是积极投身

历史的指令。*

"积极？你的意思是？"

大海边缘的光辉

经过一番淬炼

更加精纯，依稀介于

平衡与虚空之间。

而我依然不能从脑海中清空

卵石缸底舒适环境里

存活的那些生命

以及那个受挫者，离水，

坚强而迷惑。

---

*我被牵掣于……"出自切斯瓦夫·米沃什的《欧洲故土》
（*Native Realm*）（加州大学出版社，1981），第125页。（此类脚
注为作者注，下同，不另标出）

契诃夫在萨哈林*

给德里克·马洪①

所以，他将还他的"医学债"。
但首先他在海边喝干邑
背对他北上要面对的一切。
他的脑袋遨游，自由得如秋明的

三驾马车，他凭栏俯瞰
他的三十年，看入自心
一英里，仿佛他是清澈的水：
从汽船甲板望见的贝加尔湖。

那么北，西伯利亚都成了南方。
莫斯科文人送给他干邑
伴他前往流放地的征途——
他，你可以说，生于暗中交易？

---

*契诃夫前往萨哈林监狱岛的前夜，朋友们送给他一瓶干邑
白兰地。在这座岛上，契诃夫度过一八九〇年的夏天，其间采
访了所有罪犯和政治犯。他关于罪犯流放地状况的书出版于
一八九五年。
① 德里克·马洪（Derek Mahon, 1941–2020），爱尔兰诗人。

假如那美酒成为口中的溃疡，

至少那意味着他知道其价值。没有领唱人

从圣像屏帏旁的放歌

获得比他饮酒时更神圣的快乐，

那酒杯闪烁温热，如钻石温热

在沙龙中青春诱人的乳沟，

不可冒犯且明知故犯。

他感到酒杯在午夜阳光中变冷。

当他摇晃起身把酒杯砸碎在石头上

响声清脆如囚犯的锁链

萦绕他。在未来的年月

响声还将持续如他自由的负担

尝试发出正确音调——不是传单，不是论文——

离开鞭打的场面。他曾想榨干

他的奴隶血以唤醒自由人

却如影尾随囚犯向导走过萨哈林。

砂岩纪念品

一种白垩质红褐色

硬葫芦，沉积而成，

可靠密实像砖头

我常抓着它在双手间抛来抛去。

它以前更红润，有水下瘀伤的

痕迹，当我捡起它，

涉过伊尼什欧文的卵石海滩。

三角洲对面一盏盏灯光

无声地点亮拘留营

四周。来自火川佛拉革同①的石子，

在地狱火热的河床上染血？

夜晚的霜与含盐的水

让我的手蒸腾，仿佛我已拔出那颗

---

① 冥界五河之一，意为"燃烧烈焰的"，河水像是液体的火焰，
柏拉图称之为"火川"。

让盖伊·德蒙特福特*①坠入沸洪的心——

但并非如此，尽管我记得

他殉难的心在骨灰盒里，长期受敬奉。

不管怎样，当时我手中捧着

这湿润的红石，从意象和暗引的

自由邦凝望远处的瞭望塔

被双筒望远镜捕捉又放过：

一个不值得关注的剪影，

傍晚戴围巾穿水靴外出

无意于曲解或校正时代，

躬身行走，一个礼拜者。

---

* 盖伊·德蒙特福特（Guy de Montfort）。见《地狱篇》第十二歌，第118-120行；以及多萝西·塞耶斯在其译本中的注释（企鹅经典丛书）。

① 英国十三世纪贵族，为父报仇在意大利维泰博大教堂杀害表兄亨利王子（1235-1271），即亨利三世国王的侄子。在但丁《地狱篇》里，德蒙特福特因其罪行被永久罚入火川。此处的"心"和下文"殉难的心"都指亨利王子的心。

保存期限

1. 花岗岩碎片

犬牙纹石子。心灵的阿伯丁。

念着我将往杯中投一颗大珍珠[1]
我伤了我的手，太过用力按压
从乔伊斯的马泰洛塔楼敲下的
碎片，这斑驳不溶的璀璨

我留着它但少有共鸣——
石器时代的割礼刀，
我柔顺内心的加尔文锋刃。
花岗岩尖锐，咸涩，惩罚

且严厉。它说，凡劳苦负重者，
可以到我这里来，我不会
使你们恢复元气。它还说，及时
行乐。以及，你可以带走或留下我。

---

[1] 引自莎士比亚《哈姆雷特》第五幕第二景《宫中》。

2. 老熨斗

常常我看她提起它，
小巧的楔形底座
骑在火炉背上
如锚泊的拖船。

靠耳朵判断它的热度
她朝它的铁面吐口水
或把它举到脸颊边
探测它贮藏的危险。

烫衣板上柔和的砰砰。
她倾斜微凹的肘部
和专注的俯身
当她将熨斗对准亚麻布

像拿着木工刨，
像女人的怨恨。
工作，她无言的冲劲表明，
就是从一定的距离

移动一定的质量，
是全力以赴并感到
完全胜任。
感到被拖累。并浮起。

3. 旧锡盘

不是白银时代，而是
房椽下文盲人家的碎片：
一个凹陷的祖传青灰盘
布满风暴冰雪，染污而温和。

我爱低调的锡，金属中
我容易的选择——仅次于
一触热铁便流泪的焊料；
忧伤平静如树皮光滑的桤木

映在云雾缭绕的池塘表面
一个冬日他们以为我淹死在那里，
离家仅有一步之距，那时整个
村子都是雾。我故意藏起来。

微明是灵魂的构成。

迷蒙的挑战，遥远的良知光亮

与真爱畏畏缩缩、半真半假的承诺。

还有祖先的冰释姗姗来迟。

4. 道 钉

多么像一颗耙钉

我甚至听见耕地里传来

马具的吱吱和石子的哒哒。

但那是蒸汽时代

鹰潭，新罕布什尔，

我在那儿发现这生锈的铁钉

曾被对准钉入

为修复铁轨上的齿轮。

什么能保证事物的持续

如果铁轨被拔起

就像从阴沟植被里拔出长长荆棘？

我感觉与自己邂逅

在草木丛生的幽径

拔出铁钉像拔出一根刺

或一个词，我以为是我的，

却出自陌生人之口。

而那把锤头呢，伴着

最后的闷响将它钉入

杂酚油处理过的

枕木，它在哪儿？

那汗湿的锤柄呢？

问转向架上的人们，

无声且正直

疾驰而过，无影无踪。

5. 来自德尔斐的石头

在某个黎明被带回神殿

大海向南铺展它寥远的阳光麦浪

而我再度献出清晨的祭品：

愿我避开流血的腥气，

管辖舌头，畏惧傲慢，畏惧神

直到他在我无拘无束的口中说话。

6. 雪 鞋[①]

雪鞋的环挂在我脑海中的

一面墙，在一间寂如积雪的房间：

好像一个手写的毛笔字，

适用于所有耳语国度的象形文。

为追随一个词语的雪雁

我在一场爱欲风暴后离开房间，

像一个梦游人爬上阁楼楼梯，

裹着皮毛，热血沸腾，厮打雪片。

然后我坐在那儿写作，在无声中想象

声音就像长久禁欲后爱的声响，

热切、沉浸并胜任

在墙上的雪鞋符号下。

---

① 雪靴，历史悠久，遍布欧美和亚洲，是一种套在普遍鞋子下
面的防滑板，通常比普通鞋底大很多，木框结构，中间由线绳
编织为网格状，上方有绳索套在脚上。形似羽毛球拍。

雪鞋的环，像一个旧时的风筝，
在风中飘升并从视野中消失。
现在我茫然坐着，晨光渐渐照亮
它疏远而凛然的浩瀚。

迁 徙

往前走大约一英里
超出我们家的范围，
在一个屋顶漏雨、
天窗破裂的房子里
布里吉德搬来
与妈妈、姐妹同住。

此后几个月里
她睡在拥挤的床上
在树枝鞭打的石瓦下，
夜夜因初为女人
而困惑不已，
还有一个梦困扰她，

梦见一艘轮船的旅客休息室里
随着每一次缓慢的颠簸和沉浮，
空瓶子滚来滚去，
一个哭泣的孩子不停
哭泣，一辆奇怪的
漂浮的黑色出租车驶

入被轰炸的车站。
婴儿衣服的气味，
紧紧依偎的孩子，
以及开始泛白的
没有窗帘的小天窗，
这些都会让她醒来。

那些日子被风吹落的果实
躺在我脚边，秘密的风
在我们的抒情树林中微动：
静止、敏捷而沉默的
诗之鹿站在泓泓
光辉的声音中

伺机惊吓，
当晨晨昏昏
布里吉德和姐妹们
叮叮当当走来，走下
陡峭的山丘取水，
然后再吃力地上去。

精灵们！那洒落的水
在尘土中留下一条踪迹，
摇摇晃晃的白瓷桶

隐约可见。他们的幽灵，

如他们的姓名，从山间呼唤

"快点"，快过去，

洒落音节一串。

我知道当时的故事。

乘渡轮从格拉斯哥到贝尔法斯特，

然后坐火车到都柏林

带着行李和纸箱，

婴儿车和录音机，

然后他们误了公交车，

到威克洛的最后一程——

孩子们又怕又恼

在亮灯的汽车站，

母亲茫然失措。

于是绝望中

他们徒步走向郊区

直至凌晨时分。

多么甜美又是多么不安！

当他们开启思家的旅程

月光下的迁徙，街头流浪儿，

母亲和女儿们

一路往南穿过农田

经过霓虹闪烁的车库，

夜灯映在卷帘上的光环，

上锁的入口，鼓涨的

小桥及下方溪涧

亲切的呢喃，然后树木

开始填满天宇

房屋渐少渐稀，

街灯的间隔变宽

直到冰冷的月光

映照出威克洛山间

漆黑的天际线，他们坐下。

他们更换磁带

但电池没电了。

没有一丝音响。

当最初的雨滴

落入黑暗，布里吉德

起身说，"快走。"

最后的目光

悼念 E.G.^①

我们遇见他，静止
且旁若无人，
凝望一片
开花的土豆田，
他的裤脚湿了
沾满草籽。
被加冕的大头野草
在路边疯长
鞭打我们的汽车
但他仿佛听不见，
在崖顶的金钟花旁
陷入长久的注视。

那天他什么都不关心，
仿佛他是一片
挂在铁丝网上的羊毛
或一缕陈旧的干草
从过往的货车

---

① 指爱德华·伽利赫（Edward Gallagher）。

落在路边的树丛。

他回到二十多岁时，

开着杂货车

穿行多尼戈尔

伽利赫父子

商人，酒馆老板，

零售和进口。

面粉袋，饲料袋，供马

使用的水桶

在每一个白石灰的院子里。

假如他遇见一辆福特

那就是树篱间的好戏。

假如妮芙①骑马而来

用迷人的爱尔兰语

甜蜜宽广的海滨，

在潮湿而耀眼的

蹄音与蹄痕之间

蜿蜒而行，

---

① 妮芙，爱尔兰传说中海神的女儿，骑马穿越西海，诗人莪相的恋人。莪相从马上跌落，触到爱尔兰土地，变成老人。

我想甚至她也不能

使他抽身于

凝视的密林。

回忆马里布

给布赖恩·摩尔[①]

你门前的太平洋更野更冷
超出我对"太平"的设想

那好极了，因为在我想象的
微温海滨我会烂掉的。

然而它的冷绝不清苦
不似我们那僧侣钓鱼、冰雪覆盖的大西洋；

没有人给你蜂巢屋
唯有马里布的抽象沙滩——

那是早期蒙德里安和他的沙丘
在迷蒙中趋向理想形式

尽管，当风与海的喧嚣增强，
风海如万马齐嘶。

---

① 希尼的朋友，小说家。一九七〇年左右希尼曾在他马里布的
家中做客。

我活生生地在那里
在我曾想象自己可能在的地方

并经历白昼的呼啸：
但为什么它并不打动我？

大西洋的风暴已剥落
大斯凯林岛上的斗室，礁岩台阶

我不曾攀爬
它们衔接着墓园与船坞

也牢牢缝在我鞋底。
且抬起、踢掉并抛开那只鞋——

在另一个西部海边
远离斯凯林岛屿，远离，远离

冬日积水冲刷地面的声音，
我们的脚步填满飞沙。

陌生化

我站在他们之间，
一个拥有见多识广的才智
和皮革黄的自足，
言谈如铮铮弓弦，

另一个，不修边幅且一脸困惑
踩着威灵顿高靴的双筒，
面对我带来的陌生人，
微笑向我求援。

然后一个狡黠的中间音
从马路对面的田野传来
说，"熟练些，讲方言，
说说这拂过铁皮屋的风，

唤我雨后多花蔷薇
或雾中变冷的雪果。
但要爱这见多识广者的风度

也要叫我波阿斯的麦田①。

超越可靠事物，

所有那些持续的诉求，

眼睛、水洼和石子，

想想当初你多么勇敢

当我第一次拜访你

你已做出种种义无反顾的别离。"

一只苍头燕雀从桦树中跃出，然后

我发现自己竟开车带这位陌生人兜风，

走遍我的家乡，熟练地

讲方言，历数我所知的

全部值得骄傲的事情，它们就在这

历数中变得陌生。

---

① 源自《路得记》的典故。

出生地①

一

他曾写作的松木桌，那么小而简朴，

单人床，一场自律的梦。

楼下的石板厨房，微尘弥漫的斜斜

粗粗的光束：他过着不受打扰、真实可靠的

幽灵生活，无须编造。

还有房屋周围的高树，日夜

被风吹拂，缓慢得像从市场

晚归的牛车，或小提琴

在他不情愿的心里引起的颤动。

二

那天，我们就像他笔下

某对不幸的恋人，一言不发

直到他为我们说话，

---

① 此诗是希尼拜访英国作家托马斯·哈代的故居后所作。

正午沉寂的出没者
走在充满蕨类和蝴蝶的
撩人深巷，

惊惶于我们的伤痛，
在咽痛与中暑的驱使下
进入地表潮湿的树林

在那里我们制造了一段
自己的插曲，难以忘怀，
难以启齿，

然后突然钻出来像牛
钻出灌木，湿透而愤怒，
距房屋只有几步路。

三

遍布各处即无处，
谁能证明
一处比另一处更好？

我们归来空空，

既滋长又抵抗

关于停息的话语。

出生地，屋顶横梁，白石灰，

石板，壁炉，

像凌乱的铁砝码

飘浮在星系。

不过，是三十年前吗？

我第一次读书

读到第一抹曙光，为了

看完《还乡》？

再生草中的长脚秧鸡

证实它自己，我还听见

鸡鸣和犬吠，完全一样，

仿佛出自他的手笔。

变　易

当你默默随我来到
高高草丛中的水泵边

我听见许多你听不见的声音：
铁锹陷入土地的咬啮，

泥瓦匠搅拌灰浆时的
滑音和怨言，

女人提着白水桶走来
仿佛她们起伏羽翼上的闪灯。

我掀开水泵盖
铸铁边沿叮当，

有什么在它口中颤动。
我鸟瞰到一只鸟，

雀绿色，夹杂白斑，
在枯叶上筑巢，平伏，安静，

忍受这光亮。
于是我盖上这堡垒的屋顶

尽可能轻柔，并告诉你，
你也轻柔地揭开它

但鸟儿去哪了？
只有一颗蛋，卵石白，

在生锈的喷水口弯曲处
小鸟展开尾羽静静坐着。

如此温柔，我说，"记住这里。
重走这条路对你有好处

当你长大远走高飞并终于站在
这空虚城市的中心。"

阿尔斯特的暮色

裸露的灯泡，零散的铁钉，
架上的木材，闪光的凿子：
在波纹铁棚里
埃里克·道森俯向木工刨

在平安夜的五点钟。
接着是木工铅笔，辐刨，
线锯，螺旋钻，锉和锥，
再用亚麻油抹布擦拭。

一英里外它在成形，
一艘玩具战舰的骨架，
当水桶结冰，寒霜
凝固屋顶和门柱的寂静。

此刻他在哪儿？
我们俩相差十五岁
那晚我努力想听见想象中
雪橇的铃声却听见他骑车

进入我们的小巷，在山墙边下来，
把他的兰令自行车停靠
在白灰墙边，站住确认
房屋静谧，然后敲门

把他的包裹递给一个窥探的女人：
"我想你以为我永远不会来。"
埃里克，今晚我看到那一切
就像你作坊墙上的影子，

嗅探板凳下的刨花，
掂量我柔软手中冰冷的
螺丝扳手，然后站在路上
注视你摇曳的尾灯淡出

并知道如果我们重逢
在阿尔斯特的暮色中，我们可以
在一场全是玩具和木工的言谈中
任意开始并任意结束，

在门口礼让以避开
你父亲的制服和手枪，
但——既然我已经说了出来——
或许那也不会更糟。

路上的蝙蝠

一个蝙蝠似的灵魂在黑暗、秘密和孤独中觉知
自身。[1]

你总是用耙尖举起一顶旧帽子
并沿着桥洞拖行，为了搜寻微小的
蝙蝠撞击和扑动。瘦削、毛茸茸的翼膜，

幼爪抓挠帽子的防汗带……但别
把它弄下来，别再打断它的飞行，
别拒绝它；这一次给它自由。

跟随蝙蝠翅膀的拍动，在石桥下，
在米德兰与苏格兰铁路[2]下
然后让它消失在那里的黑暗中。

接下来它会投影于月光擦亮的月桂
或掠过网球场的围网。

---

① 引自詹姆斯·乔伊斯的《一个青年艺术家的画像》。
② 简称 LMS，一家英国铁路公司。

接下来它就在你的路前方了。

你在追逐什么？你不断变换方向，

盲目地飞过灰烬坑和铁丝网；

诱于诸如"女性晨衣"①一词的轻抚，

塞窣与窥探，闪光绸，鬼鬼祟祟的激流

离我这么近我能听见她的喘息

然后在那边树后亮着灯的窗前

它挂在砖墙上的匍匐植物间

时而像一片湿叶飘荡在路上，

时而如柔软毛边的影子旋花

在白门旁。谁会想到它呢？在白门旁

她让他们为所欲为。粘在那儿吧，

想要多久就多久。没有什么要隐藏。

---

① 原文 peignoir，源自法语。

给凯瑟琳·安①的榛木棍

鲑鱼鲜明的珍珠母光泽
刚露出水面

就那样消失了，但你的木棍
依然葆有鲑鱼银。

风干且柔韧，
它让手相信

你掌握你拥有的，
去玩耍去摆弄

去猛击。
但它也指向牛儿

指向噼啪和敲击
栅栏门的声音——

_____

① 希尼的小女儿。

我们可能从你的家族树
砍下的那种木棍。

一只鲜艳的钴蓝色午后蜻蜓
最初将我的目光引向它

而我为你削剪它的那个晚上
你见到你的第一只萤火虫——

我们全都默然伫立，就连你
也庞大得足以黯淡一只

萤火虫的天空。
而当我拨开草丛

一个辉耀的小窝照亮眼睛
就在你木棍粗钝的底端。

给迈克尔和克里斯托弗①的风筝

整整那个星期天下午
风筝飞越星期天，
一张绷紧的鼓面，满怀吹飞的谷壳。

我看过它制作中的灰暗和打滑，
我轻拍它当它干透变白变硬，
我把报纸做的蝴蝶结系于
它六英尺的尾巴。

但它一会儿在高空像一只小黑云雀
一会儿又拖行仿佛它涨满的牵引线
是一条湿漉漉的绳索被拉动
以便举起渔获。

我的朋友说，人的灵魂
大约就是一只鹬的重量，
然而泊在那里的灵魂，
那垂下又升起的线绳，

———————
① 迈克尔和克里斯托弗是希尼的两个儿子。

重如一条犁沟升入苍穹。

在风筝一头栽进树林
及牵线失效之前
用你们的双手抓住它吧，孩子们，感受
悲伤那弦振、根深、长尾的牵引。
你们天生适合它。
站在这儿，在我面前，
承受这拉力。

铁路儿童

当我们爬上路堑的斜坡
我们的眼睛就与电线杆上的
白瓷杯和咝咝作响的电线持平。

像随手画的可爱线条，它们向东向西蜿蜒
数英里直到超出我们的视野，在燕子的
重压下松垂。

我们太小，以为自己不知道任何
值得知道的事。我们以为词语沿着电线走，
裹着晶莹的雨滴，

每一颗都凝结饱满的
天光，铁轨的闪烁，而我们自己
被按比例无限缩小

以至可以从针眼中穿过。

甜　豆

"思想做了什么？"

　　　　　　　　　　"插

一根羽毛在地里并想着

它会长成一只母鸡。"

　　　　　　　　一杆

接一杆我们丈量甜豆垄

并钉上轻巧脆弱的木棍，

在新鲜的沃土里显得纤细违和，

然后一茎茎我们剪去

即将绽放的花蕾。

　　　　于是当疼痛

撕裂她一贯的纯洁凝视

我伸手去拿麦秸并想到：

透过蔓生植被看天，

就像绿蛛网中的水，

开出一片空地，在那里她的心歌唱，

不必戒备或尴尬，一两次。

布伦的幻象

又要到我们朝思暮想的时候了
想念北岸那鳗鱼丰美的
浅滩和沙丘，它的红藻它的海鸟，
它那被咸水逼疯的青草
其分界漫过堤坝以保护
温良者统治下的再生草。
最纯洁与最悲伤者
也有望被顾及。

从那些场景之外她抵达，不是从海贝
而是被圣埃尔莫湿冷的火焰舔舐，
最后一刻的天使，教导我们
岩石中的鱼，裂隙深处
蕨类植物迷茫的温柔。

那天我们攀登时
石子的咔哒是一场布道
宣讲良心与治愈，
她的泪滴是灾难现场
受惊的小鹿。

赤颈鸭

给保罗·马尔登[①]

它被严重射伤。
当他拔它的毛时
他发现，他说，鸭的喉——

像一枚笛音栓
塞住残破的气管——

于是吹奏它
出人意外
他自己的小赤颈鸭悲啼。

---

① 爱尔兰诗人，一九五一年生。

希拉纳吉

在基尔佩克

一

我们仰望她
以她的角度蹲在
屋檐下。

她用腰背和肩膀
以及被缚的双肘
承担起整块石头的重负，

狡黠的嘴，抓紧的手指
在说插啊，使劲儿插啊，
再使劲儿些。

屁股高高的，
她的大蝌蚪额头
圆圆地凸显在阳光中。

而她身旁有两只鸟，

一个兔子头，一个山羊的，
一张吞噬很多头的口。

二

她用双手支撑自己
像老谷仓里一双手
撑开一只麻袋。

我从外面向里看
看那交叠而柔软的口
流泻谷粒。

我仰望茅屋顶下
鸟窝或鼠洞的
黑暗的口和眼，

闻墙上的蔷薇，
霉，泥土地，
温暖的屋檐深处。

然后一天晚上在院子里
我站在大雨中一动不动
头顶麻袋如发网。

三

我们瞻仰她，
她圆垒的眼睛，
她小而圆滑的肩，

她缺裂扁平的鼻子，
并在瞻仰中感到眩晕。
她骨如细枝，骑马做爱，

变得成熟，变得普通，
仿佛在说，
"是啊，尽情地看我吧

但也看看其他东西。"
一个穿格裙的跳跃者，
两个接吻的人，

一张衔小枝的嘴，
一只奔跑的雄赤鹿，两条鱼，
一头被毁的持乐器的野兽。

小　路

一

当我走下这条小路
树篱间游移的风就像
老人呼啸的言语。而我知道
我处在失落语词的灵泊。

它们飞到那里，从橡棚和十字路口，
从山墙端的荫蔽和废弃的马车。
我看见它们涌出桦木白的咽喉
在铁床架上方振翅盘旋
直到灵魂脱离肉体。
然后有一天，近得如同陌生人的呼吸
它们如烟云升起在夏日的天空
并安顿在石头的小舌
以及山楂的软肺。

于是我知道了为什么从一开始
这条小路就吹拂我，甚至现在也吹着
在珠尘游丝的震颤中
在最后几朵山楂花和玫瑰果的咳血中。

二

大嗓门在没有女人的厨房里。

他们在夏季从不开灯

而是凭借降临的暮色

如同庄严的树林。他们一直坐在黑暗中，

口中的烟斗通红，言谈少到

重复的是啊是啊，当狗挪动，

短促地说乖伙计！我闭上眼睛

好让光的微尘在眼帘后流过

我的头轻飘，我的椅子

在树枝间忽高忽低而风

以又一声长长的是啊惊动鸦群。

三

默立。你会听见

万物的音响。高压线缆

在牛群、拖拉机、叫唤的狗、

一英里外换挡的重型货车之上歌唱。

而永远有大地表面的喧嚣，

你不知道你听见，直到嫩枝折断

以及一只乌鸫受惊的鸣啭

戛然而止。

     当你累了或怕了
你的声音悄悄回到它原初的地方
并发出你的幽魂在那里发出的声响……
当但丁从流血的树上折断嫩枝
汩汩的鲜血中传来一声叹息
像燃烧的青枝尖梢流出的汁液。

如今听到某处狱锁的咔嗒
审问者磨砺他的《进堂咏》，
光的微尘燃烧，血红的香烟
惊扰幽魂，尖叫并哀求。

采砂场

1. 一九四六

第一个洞像活板门一样整齐

被割入草地

再割一次，当铁铲开始

挥舞，刀片摩擦卵石，

手柄的震动减弱，

在驱动的刀刃中遭遇

小小报应。

            蠕虫与星光，

泥浆在骑单车的路人脸上。

老鼠的鼻子在灰泥路边嗅探，

他们走去那里清洁靴子。

2. 复员的瓦匠

篱笆桩被整修安放

入位，但格格不入：

士兵

不再是士兵且从来

不算是士兵，他走进了

什么地方？不是荒漠

之夜，冰冷的救护车聚集，

不是全世界的终极

沙漠，太阳的金鞭

和烤架——

　　　　　这片沙，

这沉重大地的光辉

是贪婪的铜币钉在

传说中的许愿树，

金钱的湿矿砂。

　　　　　长满晒斑，

退伍复员，他劳作不辍

像他吸入的泥土，他站着

忆起他的行当，抹刀

修琢砖头时的歌声，

刀柄的啪嗒声，铅锤线的

确信，酒精水准仪

眼里的欢乐。

3.沙的暴发

财富在沙中。沙坑与沙堤。

河里的沙砾在砖厂晾干。

结土痂的燧石，打水漂的瓦砾，

砂岩的卵石，斑驳如鸟蛋的花岗岩

全都在混凝土搅拌机结块的

铁口中咯咯作响。

　　　　　　只见第一铲

被铲起，我把一捧沙砾

扔进货料槽，

直到它们烧成火球

或在爆炸边缘碎裂

或在被夷平的地带再度饮雨，

被砌合并准备记录

任何进入墙体的房梁和脉动。

像不死的谷粒在搁浅的蛤壳。

巨砾在瀑布后倾听。

以及：

　　　　毛地黄和幼苗

在完工后的井底，青草在裂开的

地表，垂钓者栖在深涧上方

杂草丛生的卸货台。

4. 砖石保存了什么

他的触摸，他关于坦克的白日梦，
他在脚手架上的制高点
俯瞰正午的烟囱和近处的山峦，
隐秘的河水发出持续的声响
一片新住宅区拔地而起——
抹刀一挥，他就把这一切
永远地封进砖石。
这还没有结束
这只是此后一切的先锋：
被锤打的地板，水管最初的
汩汩涌流，电话线和山墙上
飘扬的旗帜，床头板
发出快速的撞击，砰然关上的门撼动
托梁，让屋顶的蓄水池泛起涟漪。
而我自己的双手，小孙儿的手那么大，
进到那里，又冷又湿，而我立刻
睁大眼睛凝视砂井。

渠堤之王 *

给约翰·蒙塔古①

一

仿佛一个闯入者
打开一扇被遗忘之门
扯掉缠绕在栅栏
下方的杂草——

就在树篱那边
他沿着河岸解开一条
黑暗的摩尔斯电码，
一道弯曲的伤疤

那沉默的蛛网般的
青草。我停下
他也停下
像月亮。

---

* 见本书第三部分注释。
① 约翰·蒙塔古（1926–2016），诗人，生于纽约，在爱尔兰长大。

他活在他的双脚

和耳朵里，善察天气，

潜行谛听，

一个无穴的游移者。

在桥下

他的倒影随水流

移至边缘，

蛾飞，诱人。

我被他那

隐秘的足音纠缠，

出人意料的足迹，

落定的花粉。

二

我确信我认识他。那些痴迷的阁楼时光，我努力
让自己接近他：每一个着迷的间隙，我一根接一
根地吸烟，凝望天窗外长满草的山坡，将自己暴
露无遗。他依赖我，当我孤身悬于一个移译的
词组，像小孩冒险挂在旋涡上方的桤木枝。枝
叶间小小的梦幻自我。我俯向梦幻恐惧，盘问：

——你是我跑上楼却发现淹死在浴缸流水下的
　　那个吗？
——是被割草机割断的那个吗，像僵硬的丰收
　　浮雕中的野兔？
——我们把他染血的小衣服埋在花园的那个？
——在黑夜中无眠，与不安的马蹄声仅一墙之
　　隔的那个？

在斗胆发出这些呼唤后，我转身走向大门跟随
他。隐秘行动是我的第二天性，仿佛我正在进
入我自身。我记起我曾被授予这天职。

三

那天当我被带到一边
我有一种被选中之感：

他们用渔网装饰我的头
并将叶茂的细枝织入网孔

于是我的视野是丛林
深处鸟儿的目光

我边走边说
像战栗的灌木发出的语声。

我，渠堤之王，
顺从地跟随他们

来到鸽林的边缘——
落叶的树冠，暮色中有篷的干草车

我们沉默地躺在下面。
没有鸟来，但我等着

在荆棘和石子之间，或低语
或碰破迷濛的游丝

若我动一动肌肉。
"回到我们中来，"他们说，"丰收时，

当我们藏在谷堆里，
当猎狗几乎无法取回

被击落的东西。"而我看见自己
在伪装中起身行进，

结着顶髻，麦捆遮脸，留心

鸟儿们的坠落：一个富有的年轻人

离开他拥有的一切

赴一场候鸟式的孤独。

第二部分：斯泰森岛 *

---

* 一组与熟悉亡魂的梦中邂逅，发生在多尼戈尔郡德格湖上的斯泰森岛。该岛也称为"圣帕特里克的炼狱"，因为传统认为，帕特里克最先建立了斋戒和祈祷的忏悔守夜仪式，如今依然是为期三日的朝圣的基本内容。当代朝圣者礼拜仪式的每个单元称为一个"圣地礼忏"（station），每个"圣地礼忏"的很大一部分内容包括环绕"基座"（环形石基，据说是中世纪早期僧侣斗室的残余部分）赤脚行走和祈祷。

第二部分　工作原理探索

斯泰森岛

一

一阵匆匆的钟声

掠过清晨的寂静

和起水泡的麦田，

一种遁去的鸣响

突然停息正如

它突然而来。礼拜天，

静寂呼吸

且无法平息

因为有个人出现

在那片田野边

拿着弓锯，僵直

举起如里拉琴。

他走走停停并抬头

凝视那片榛树丛，

把锯斜斜插入，

抽出再凝视

然后继续下一个。
"我知道你，西蒙·斯威尼，
违背安息日的惯犯
已死去多年。"

"你知道个鬼，"他说，
目光依然在树篱
头也不回。
"我曾是你的神秘人
今早又是了。

透过灌木的缝隙，
你初领圣餐的脸
总是看我伐木。
当砍下或折断的
树枝变黄，当

木烟磨砺空气
或沟渠沙沙作响
你觉察到我的踪迹
仿佛那儿被撒尿圈地。
这让你有些恐惧。

当他们命你

在卧室的黑暗中
谛听树间的风雨
并想象游走的补锅匠
露宿在倾斜的货车下

你闭上眼睛看见
月光中湿漉漉的
轮轴和轮辐，而我
浑身淌着雨水，
正走向你的家门。"

阳光闯入榛林，
急切的钟声再次
响起。我转向
另一种声音：
一群戴头巾的女人

正涉过幼嫩的麦田，
她们的裙摆轻拂。
她们的仪态悲伤了晨曦。
它向静寂低语，
"为我们祈祷，为我们祈祷，"

它对空念咒召唤

直到田野上满是

依稀记起的脸孔，

一群松散的会众

三三两两地走过。

当我拖步跟随

我是斋戒的朝圣者，

头晕脑胀，离家

去直面我的圣地。

"远离一切游行！"

斯威尼朝我大喊，

但人群的低语

和他们沙沙踩过

柔嫩草叶的脚步

辟出一条下了迷药的路

我被迫踏上它。

我追踪那些早起者

他们早在炊烟升起前

就步调一致地出发。

急切的钟声再度轰鸣。

二

我在高速公路上停车，聆听
凤头麦鸡和车外呼啸的风
这时后视镜里突然出现了什么，

是一个人快步走来，穿着大衣
和高靴，没戴帽子，魁梧，坚决，
以确定而匆忙的步履沿路拱走来

以至于我觉得自己受到了挑衅。
车门砰地关上。我突然来到车外
与一个恼怒的人面面相觑

他愤然谈起多少个夜晚，
侧耳倾听枪托猛敲门板，
暴动的自耕农，他的邻居

也在其中，竭力说清事物的真相。
"你就在这里赶上了那些女人，"
我说，这很显然。"你的《德格湖朝圣者》

萦绕我心，每当我穿越这座山峰——

仿佛我被什么跟踪，或在跟踪着什么。

我正在忏悔朝圣的途中。"

"哦，神圣的耶稣基督，难道什么都没变吗？"

他使劲儿摇头又抬起来

像潜水员浮出水面，

然后带着一种"这毛头小子究竟

是谁"的神情，他再次留意

他所在之处：道路，山顶，

和天空，在雨中变得柔和，

显著地平息了他的愤怒，直到：

"这条路你必须自己走。

我，曾在亚麻的臭味中识字

闻过绞刑架上腐尸的气息

也看过他们的黏液环绕麻袋闪烁——

倔强的绿带会和奥兰治偏执狂

让我成为说谎的老叛徒

弄脏他们政治的牛棚。

如果时世强硬，我也会强硬。

我让我身上的背叛者插入刀锋。

也许你可以从中吸取教训，

无论你是谁，无论来自哪儿，

因为，尽管你笑得自然

我还是从中感到一种戒备。"

"我不适合扮演愤怒的角色，"

我说，"我来自德里郡，

出生地距天主教堂一步之遥

那里绿带会乐队为圣母奏响赞歌。

那时兄弟会已是脆弱的队伍

在帕特里克节喝醉踉跄回家

戴着绿边的蕾丝领和绶带。

他们顺从的曲调最初吸引我

而不是芬尼亚党人拨响的

不依不饶的铁竖琴。你写的很多事

我都听过做过：德格湖这圣地，

拔亚麻，跳舞，夏日十字路口的闲谈

以及地方教育的战栗乡音。

所有那些。而且，永远都有奥兰治鼓。

还有邻居们夜晚持枪在街头。"

"我知道，我知道，我知道，我知道，"他说。

"但你必须努力去理解发生的事情。
记住一切并保持清醒。"

"树篱中的桤木，"我说，"蘑菇，
牛马排粪的丛丛幽草，
带衬膜的栗壳在你掌中裂开的

咯咯声，腐烂果壳的消融，
被淤泥阻塞的排水沟里的旧果酱罐——"
但这时卡尔顿*打断我说：

"这一切就像养在泉水里的鳟鱼
或撒在伤口里的蛆虫——
另一种生命净化我们的环境。

我们是大地的地虫，而所有那些
经过我们的将成为我们的踪迹。"
说这话时他迅速向后转身

并以同样坚实的步伐继续向前。

_____

*威廉·卡尔顿（William Carleton，1794–1869），生来是天主
教徒，少年时期完成朝圣，改宗英国国教后，在《德格湖朝圣
者》中发表了对这一朝圣的批评，并以其最著名的作品《爱尔
兰农民的特点和故事》（*Traits and Stories of the Irish Peasantry*，
1830–1833）开启事业生涯。

三

我跪下。间歇。习俗之遗风……
我回到念珠的嗒嗒和忏悔室里
传来的低语中，侧边祭坛上
熄灭的蜡烛散发淡淡的

亲密的体温般的蜡油味。
一种活跃的、让风平息的寂静，仿佛
海螺中被侧耳倾听的海音停歇
而浪潮凝滞并支撑屋顶。

然后一个海边饰物漂浮并闲荡
在视野中，像闪着磷光的野草，
一个玩具神龛，上面用幼蚌
和鸟蛤的贝壳拼贴出图案，

珍珠从一个病童的气息中凝结
为一艘闪光的方舟，我的黄金屋
容纳着久远以前她死时雪花莲盛开的
节气。我会躲进我们大橡木

餐具柜的货舱里搜寻它

永久地包着纸巾放在一边。

那就像触摸鸟蛋，从鸟巢中

劫掠花环一词，珍藏、干燥、秘密

如几乎从不提起的她的名

却是一只困在我体内的白鸟

拍打受惊的翅膀，当病人之痙

在连祷文中战栗地说出为我等祈祷。

一阵冷风吹过跪垫下方。

我想起不断

环绕一个空间，绝对空无，

绝对之源，如同声音的理念；

如同一种缺席驻留在以沼泽为食的空中

下方是一圈被踩倒的青草和灯芯草

我们曾在那里发现数周前消失的

我们那条狗的腐尸和毛发。

四

模糊的眩晕，当我面朝太阳，背
对石柱和铁十字，
准备说那些梦话我放弃……

新入圣职者模糊的椭圆形肖像，
带着讨好的意味说出的"神父"，
父母被祝福时阳光照耀的泪珠。

我遇见一年轻牧师，油光如乌鸫，
仿佛他刚刚从他的涂油礼
移开：他的紫色圣带和饰绳

或腰带松松系着，他锃亮的鞋子
在打褶蕾丝边的白色亚麻圣衣下
出乎意料地世俗。

他的名字多年来无人搅扰
像阴沟里的旧自行车轮
终于在丛生的灌木下破裂，

受潮并消亡。我的双臂敞开

但我无法说出那些话。"雨林，"他说，
"你从没见过那样的场景。我维持了

仅仅一两年。袒胸的
女人和鼠肋的男人。一切都白费了。
我像一颗梨烂掉。我汗如雨下……"

他的呼吸越来越短促。"在长屋里
我把圣杯举过头巾。
见此标志……在那废弃的

传教团院落，我的使命
是湿透的攀缘植物上的水气。"
他说话时，我中止了我的

弃世声明，以便让路给
其他排队等候的朝圣者。
"如今我比你当年离开时年纪还大。"

我斗胆说，感到一种奇怪的反转。
"我无法见到你在异域传教。
我只看到你骑着单车，

一个回家过暑假的神学院学生

注定要从事体面的工作。访邻。
品茶并称赞自制的面包。

他们心中的某些东西将得到认可
当他们看到你一袭黑衣站在门口,
如某种神圣的吉祥物莅临。

你给予莫大安慰,你解除世界
对他们的包围——围攻其厨房里
挂满圣像和十字架的神龛。"

"你呢,"他支吾地说,"你在此做的
不是同一回事?你着了什么魔?
至少我当时年少无知

不知道我所谓的被选中不过是惯例。
但这一切你已被豁免却依旧重蹈
覆辙。而神,据说,已经撤退。

你在做什么,经历这些流程?
除非……除非……"他再次呼吸短促
且整个发烧的身体变黄并颤抖。

"除非你来这儿是为了看最后一眼。"

突然间他所站之处空荡如我俩
长大时附近的道路，那里有个病人

在一个细雨之夜看了最后一眼
那时水气蒸腾如春天最初的呼吸，
一场及膝的迷雾中我默默跋涉

在他身后，他在巡回布道，探访。

五

老人的手，像柔软的爪子向前划动，
摸索并避让前方的空气。
巴尼·墨菲①拖着脚步走在混凝土路上。
墨菲老师。我听见虚弱的嗓音
在勃然大怒中再度吼叫
便跟在他身后，眼睛盯着他的脚跟
像一个拾草者尾随除草机的脚跟。
他没穿袜子的脚仿佛干蚕豆
在旧教室窗口高悬的陈列罐里
绷开它身上的缝线，
苍白如教室门内羞涩的脸。
"老师，"那些年纪稍大的低声说，"请问，老师……"
把信封弄得沙沙作响，递交，收回，
而我自言自语重复着"老师"
以至于他停下但没有转身或移动，
他的肩膀安静而瘦小，他的头
在湖面的冷风中变得警觉。
我走上前面对他，握他的手。

---

① 希尼的小学校长。

翼领之上，他那生斑的脸
在微笑中远去，当他准备
发声，嘶哑，刺耳。"很好，
你很好。"然后话音又落入
咽喉的灵泊与枯瓮。
喉结在饱经风霜的喉囊中
运作就像活塞在干涸的水泵中
对于那无助的微笑却爱莫能助。
早晨田野的气息随风袭来，
雨后多花蔷薇的性感风范，
新割的牧草，鸟巢堆满树叶。
"你会认为，安娜霍里什学校
堪称任何人的炼狱，"
我说，"你已完成了你的礼忏。"
然后一阵轻微的颤动，他的呼吸
轻柔地掠过空气如他失落草场里的镰刀。
"白桦已覆盖莱特里姆沼泽，
乳牛在学校曾在的地方吃草
学校花园的黑沃土已成牧场。"
他说完便走了，而我站错了方向，
面对更多沉迷此演练的朝圣者。
当我站在他们的低语和赤脚中
所有那些我出发和他
面对面上拉丁语课时的晨雾

令我振奋。*Mensa, mensa, mensam,*①
在空中歌唱如忙碌的磨刀石。

"有一天我们会去我叔叔在图姆的农场——"
另一位老师②说。"什么是诗歌的
伟大动力和源泉？情感，
尤其是，爱。③去年去那里时，
我从那源泉喝下三杯清水。
水很凉，刺痛我的耳朵。
你本该见见他——"像往常一样进来，
带着擦亮的引语和斜睨的鸟目
瞄准细节。当你在路上，
让人搭便车。你总会学到些什么。
他走了，穿着系腰带的华达呢，
在他身后，第三个养育者④，
肩膀松垮，目光清澈，"当然，我也许知道
一旦我开路，你早晚会

---

① 拉丁文：桌子，桌子（主格），桌子（宾格）。
② 指迈克尔·麦克莱弗蒂（Michael McLaverty，1904–1992），小说家，贝尔法斯特的圣托马斯中级学校校长，曾把帕特里克·卡瓦纳的诗集借给希尼。
③ 引自杰拉德·曼利·霍普金斯一八七九年写给罗伯特·布里奇斯的信。
④ 帕特里克·卡瓦纳（Patrick Kavanagh，1904–1967），爱尔兰诗人，代表作为《大饥荒》。

跟着我。四十二年了*

你还没有走远！但继续尾随吧，

你还能去哪儿呢？冰岛，也许？也许多尔多涅？

然后临走前甩下一句。"在我那个年代

古怪的人来这里为猎捕女人。"

---

* 四十二年了……"一九四二年，帕特里克·卡瓦纳写下他死后出版的诗《德格湖》。

六

雀斑脸，狐狸头，金雀花的荚果，

柳絮精灵，蕨草的微颤：

她从哪里来？

像一个许了

又消失的愿，我在"默祷"中选择

她并对她私语。当我们玩"过家家"。

我在大教堂门口中暑了——

遥远的寂静，空间，餐盘，

熏黑的锡罐和碰倒的板凳——

像一块被践踏的新石器时代地板

在沙丘中被揭示，弯折的草

像芦苇低语米达斯的

秘密，秘密。我拒不听钟声。

头相拥。眼紧闭。耳相贴。别说。别说。

朝圣者的人流响应钟声

疲惫地走上台阶，当我正往下走

走向那深绿的、寂静的

橡树荫。萨宾人农庄的鬼魂

在圣帕特里克炼狱的基座上。

夏末，乡村远景，没有一丝风：

解开长袍纵情诗酒

直到归来的福玻斯击溃晨星。*

当献给马利亚的赞美诗催眠地响起

我感到一种陈年旧痛，那是一袋袋

稻谷、干草叉与锄头的斜柄

曾经嘲笑我的，我自己漫长的处男

斋戒和饥渴，我每夜的阴暗宴飨，

出没于词语的谷仓比如乳房一词。

仿佛我多年来长跪在锁孔前

并为之疯狂，然后打开后的一切

不过是忏悔室被玷污的窗格，

直到那晚我透过她锁孔连衣裙

洞开的锁孔看见她蜜色肌肤的

肩胛和她背上的麦田

然后一扇朝向幸运的南方腹地的窗

打开，我吸入善意的土地。

像在夜晚寒意中全都低垂闭合的小花

一旦感到阳光的抚摸

就在茎叶上抖擞盛开，

我也在自己枯萎的力量中复苏

---

*引自贺拉斯《颂歌》第三卷，xxi，第24行。

我的心焕发光彩，像某个获释者。*

在橡树下，被移译，被给予。

---

*引自但丁《神曲·地狱篇》第二歌，第 127–132 行。

七

我已经来到这水边，
仅仅望着已令人安慰，闲视
仿佛它是清晰的晴雨表

或一面平镜，这时他的倒影
虽不显现我却感到一种在场
正在进入我的凝神

凝神于我的走神，因他唤出
我的名。而我虽不情愿
却转身面对他的脸，至今

我依然震惊于当时所见。他眼睛
上方的额头被击开，血
凝固在脖子和脸颊。"放轻松，"

他说，"只是我。你见过足球赛后
人们擦伤的样子……我被吵醒时
是几点，我现在依然不知

但我曾听见敲击、敲击，而这

令我恐惧，就像凌晨的电话，
所以直觉让我不要开灯

而是从窗帘后向外张望。
我看见门阶上有两个顾客
一辆旧越野车敞开车门

停在街上，于是我拉下窗帘；
但他们一定是在等待窗帘掀起
因为他们大喊，快下到店里来。

那时她开始哭并在床上辗转，
对着自己哀叹又哀叹，
甚至不问那是谁。'你是不是

疯了，还是发生了什么？'我咆哮，更多
是为了让自己清醒
而不是真生她的气

因为那敲击让我不宁，他们连续的敲击，
还有她不停的抱怨和近乎尖叫都让情况更糟。
他们一直在喊，'开店！

开店！'于是我穿上鞋和运动衣

回到窗边向外喊道，
'你们要干吗？能不能安静别吵

不然我就不下去了。''有个孩子不舒服。
开门看看你店里有什么——药丸
药粉或瓶装的什么药，'

其中一个说。他往人行道后退了几步
于是我看见街灯下他的脸
而当另一人移动，我认出他们两个。

但和敲击声一样糟糕的是，沉寂
更加致命。这时她平静了，
一动不动地躺着，低声说当心。

在卧室门口我打开灯。
'真奇怪，他们不去找药剂师。
三更半夜的，他们到底是谁？'

她问我，瞪目而警觉。
'我认识他们，'我说，却莫名地
越过床去握紧她的手

然后下楼来到店铺的

过道。我站在那儿，两腿
发软。我还记得开门时

传来一股熟肉或什么的
腐味。此后的事
你和我知道的一样多了。"

"他们什么都没说吗？""没有。还能说什么呢？"
"他们穿军装了吗？没有戴任何面罩吗？"
"他们毫无掩饰，就像在光天化日之下，

他妈的他们以为自己就是天下。"
"我不是要安慰你，
他们被抓了，"我告诉他，"坐牢了。"

四肢魁梧，体面，坦率，他站着
如今忘了一切，除了
被蹂躏的脑里涌起的什么回忆，

开始微笑。"你胖了，
跟那个星期天晚上你开着
租来的大奥斯汀去表白时相比。"

出生入死他几乎没有变老。

永远有一种运动员的洁净
在他身上闪耀，除了被毁的

前额和血迹，他还是那个
四肢修长的中场运动员，穿蓝色球衣
和笔挺的短裤，球队中唯一有格调的人，

完美，整洁，难以想象的受害者。
"原谅我那样冷漠地生活——
原谅我怯懦、谨小慎微的介入，"

我的话让我自己震惊。"原谅
我的目光，"他说，"这一切难以理解。"
随即一阵疼痛仿佛传遍他全身

他颤抖如一股热浪然后消失。

八

黑水。白浪。被雪覆盖的犁沟。
一只喜鹊从教堂飞来
在花岗岩的通风空间里跌撞，
我正凝视这空间，跪在
圣布里吉德忏悔座的坚硬入口。
我回过神来，在基座的石头中心
是我的考古学家，像极了他本人，
他那抄工的脸露出双唇紧闭的微笑，
一看到我就像昔日一样开始
故作惊讶，以至于他绿林好汉的
分头在脑门上散成扇形。
然后仿佛阵雨使已然乌黑的
麦茬变黑，他难言之苦的
黑天气也将他笼罩。
一个躬身低语、绕座巡行的朝圣者
从我们之间缓缓走过。

"病房里，那些在你身旁屏幕上
搏动的梦幻星辰——我是说，你的心跳，汤姆——
让我害怕，因为它们让事物裸露无遗。
那次探访中，我的玩笑早早失效。

我无法将目光从仪器上移开。

我不得不立即返回都柏林，

内疚，空虚，觉得自己什么都没说

并且，一如既往，我多少违背了

契约，没有尽到一种义务。

我隐约知道我们不会再见面……

难道我们长久的凝视和最后的握手

之中没有什么能缓解这一认识吗？"

"完全没有。但熟悉的石头

让我近乎麻木地独自面对这件事。

我爱我面无表情的考古学。

高高十字架上执拗的

面相，修道院里雕刻的头像……

不然干吗要在那坚硬的地方深掘数年

在墙下一片污浊的偏执中

在碎片和威廉派①的炮弹中挖来挖去？

但所有这些也被我们变成玩笑。

我觉得我应该更常与你见面

或许本来也会如此——但却死在三十二岁！

啊诗人，幸运的诗人，告诉我为什么

———————————

① 威廉派（Williamite），指威廉三世（亦称奥兰治的威廉，
1689–1702 年在位）的支持者。与之相对的是支持詹姆斯二世
的詹姆斯党人。

那看似应得且应许的却与我擦肩而过？

我说不出话。但见一堆黑色

玄武岩斧头，光滑如甲壳虫的背，

一个集结石力并可能引爆的石堆，

危如累卵。然后我看见一张他曾经

赠我的脸庞，一个女修道院长的

石膏铸模，是高兰镇的师傅做的，

口唇柔顺，头戴僧帽，优雅的人物。

"你的礼物将成为我们家的烛光。"

但当我张望，想与他的目光交汇时，他不见了，

取而代之蹲在那里的

是一个流血、苍白的男孩，浑身是泥。

"我被杀的那个星期天

红烫的拨火棒在哲伯恩特燃起漂亮的红光，"

他平静地说。"还记得吗？

接到消息时，你正和诗人们在一起

并继续留下来和他们一起，而你的亲骨肉

则被人用敞篷车从菲尤斯运往贝拉希。

那里的人们听到消息时比你

更激动。"

        "但他们是亲历

危机，科勒姆，他们不巧碰上

活生生的宗派暗杀。

我一时语塞，遭遇这命定的事情。"

我就这样跟我的远方表弟解释。

"我总是看到一片灰濛的贝格湖

和破晓时分空荡的湖滨。

我觉得自己就像干涸的湖底。"

"你看见那些，你写下那些——而非事实。

你混淆托辞与艺术策略。

那个开枪射穿我头颅的新教徒

我直接控诉他，但你，间接地，

或许正伏在这忏悔座上

为你的行径赎罪：你粉饰丑恶

拉起《炼狱篇》的美丽帷幕，

并用朝露美化我的死。"

然后我仿佛从睡梦中醒来

周围是更多我不认识的朝圣者

缓缓漂向客栈过夜。

九

"我的脑风干如铺开的泥炭，我的胃
萎缩成炭渣，收紧并破裂。
常常我就是那些狗舔舐
我可能舔过的湿草地上自己的血迹。
在监狱盖毯下，一种让我有安全感的
埋伏式寂静将我包围。
小镇的街灯亮了，炸弹的火光
先于声响，我看见我熟识的地带
从格伦谢恩到图姆，
听见依然可辨的多年前的汽车声，
我坐在后排像一个脸色苍白的新郎，
一个即将开枪的杀手，空虚而致命。
当警察推出我的棺材，我很轻
一如我当初瞄准时的脑袋。"

　　　　　　　　这来自枯萎病
和饥馑的声音从黑暗的宿舍消失：
他在那儿，准备殡葬的遗体，被裹尸布
包裹的脚边堆放着弥撒卡。然后是鸣枪队
在放风场的齐射。我看见木蛀虫
在大门柱和房门框里，闻到霉味
来自他观望并藏身的牛棚上的阁楼，

来自他被覆盖的灵柩将要漂过的田野。
不安的灵魂，他们本应把你埋在
你抛出第一颗手榴弹的沼泽，
那里只有直升机和杓鹬
发出它们受伤的音乐，还有泥炭藓
能够教给你疗伤的安息
直到，当鼬鼠衔着尾巴发出哨音，
再没有其他鼬鼠听从它的召唤。

我梦且游。一切仿佛都流逝荒废了
就像在污浊闪亮的洪流旋涡中
奇怪的水螅虫漂浮如一朵巨大腐烂的
木兰花，超现实如一只脱落的乳房，
我指的是我那被水流轻刷并漂白的自厌。
于是我在夜晚的水域呼喊："我忏悔
我那没有断奶的人生，它使我足以
与共谋和不信一起梦游。"
然后，像从水螅虫生出的一条雌蕊，
一根点亮的蜡烛升起并稳固
直到整个桅杆明亮的家伙重新找回
航道，它曾追随的水流
就是它行进并显露的航迹。不再漂流，
我的脚触底，我的心复活。

然后某种圆形清澈

且微荡的东西，像一个泡膜

或平滑微澜的湖面上的月亮

升起在布满蛛网的空间：一件乐器

熔化的内部光泽

朝我充分旋转它抛光的

凸面，那么近那么亮

我头朝地向后栽倒。

然后便是醒来后的澄澈

阳光、钟声和隔壁房间里水龙头

汩汩的水声。它依然在那里供人取用！

我曾在阁楼的茅草屋顶里发现的那把

旧铜号连同它的阀键和活塞，一个秘密，

曾被我退避，因为我以为如此宝物非我所有。

"我恨我那么快就知晓自己的位置。

我恨我的出生地，恨一切

让我顺从并缄口的事物。"

我对着梳妆镜中我那张

半镇定的脸张口结舌，像某个

聚会中醉倒在卫生间的人，

因看到他自己的影像而安静而厌恶。

仿佛石堆中的石砾能反抗石堆。

仿佛旋涡能改造潭水。

仿佛在小瀑布底下打转的石子，

在河床中被腐蚀且依然腐蚀着，

能把自己磨成一个不同的核。

于是我想起那个舞动不息的部落

他们一直跳舞跳到看见鹿来。

十

客栈清晨的骚动。罐子
挂在铸铁环上。煤屑。沸涨的水。
敞开的门接纳阳光。
壁炉烟游荡，陶器砰砰

如鼓音将我召回，我看见那个水杯
在我够不着的高架上，有着
矢车菊图案的那个，一条条蓝色枝蔓
反复缠绕，安静如一座里程碑，

古老，釉彩，发丝般裂痕。常年
立于它耐心的光泽与不安的原子中，
不曾挑战、不被惦念的灶神
我仿佛被它唤醒，也从它那儿醒来。

它几时不在那里的？有一天晚上
临时舞台的演员把它当作道具
而我坐在黑暗的厅堂中与它疏远
一对恋人海誓山盟将它唤作爱杯

并在我们的注目下举杯直到帷幕

猝然落下，伴着通常的噪音。

经过这次移译的洗礼和加持，

它得到复元，它全部的矢车菊雾霾蓝

依然在瞌睡，它的羊皮釉牢固——

一如罗南的诗篇在湖水下失踪

一天一夜后被水獭托出水面

奇迹般完好无损。

于是圣徒在湖畔赞美上帝。

不可能的辉耀突然

耀过门槛，太阳的强光

熄灭忠贞的微小炉火。

十一

仿佛那个被我投入

一桶浑水的万花筒棱镜

浮出水面如非凡的灯船

它淤塞的晶体中现出一张

多年前在窗格后说话的修士的脸

再度说起有必要且有可能

拯救一切，重新想象

任何被错误低估的天赋之顶点

和难得一见的璀璨……

凡落空的总会被重新充满。

"读诗如读祷文，"他说，"作为你的苦修

为我翻译些胡安·德拉·克鲁斯①的作品。"

从西班牙回到我们皴裂的荒野，

他的辅音送气，他的前额发光，

---

① 一般称作圣胡安·德拉·克鲁斯（Sun Juan de la Cruz，1542–
1591），西班牙黄金世纪经典诗人，代表作包括《灵歌》（*Cántico
espiritual*）与《灵魂的暗夜》（*La noche oscura del alma*）。

他让我觉得没有什么可忏悔。

此刻他那步履之旅激发我想到：
我多么熟知那泉水，注满，奔流，
　　　　尽管现在是黑夜。*

那永恒之泉，悄然隐匿，
我知道它的港湾它的秘密
　　　　尽管现在是黑夜。

但不知它的源头因为它没有源头，
它是一切源头的源头和本原
　　　　尽管现在是黑夜。

没有其他事物能如此美丽。
在这里，天与地畅饮至极
　　　　尽管现在是黑夜。

如此清澈，它永远不会被染污，
我也知道所有光都由此焕发而出
　　　　尽管现在是黑夜。

_____

*此节起以"黑夜"结尾的十二节即移译自胡安·德拉·克鲁斯的诗——《灵魂欣喜于以信仰知上帝之歌》(*Cantar del alma que se huelga de conocer a Dios por fe*)。

我知道没有测深线能发现它的源底，
没有人涉过或测过它的最深处
　　　尽管现在是黑夜。

而它的水流如此浩瀚以致溢出
去涤荡地狱天堂和所有民族
　　　尽管现在是黑夜。

而在那里形成的水流，
它想流多远，就能流多远
　　　尽管现在是黑夜。

而从这两股水流中涌出第三股
据我所知，非前二者所能超越
　　　尽管现在是黑夜。

这永恒之泉隐秘又飞溅
在这个我们赖以生存的生命食粮之中
　　　尽管现在是黑夜。

听它向众生发出呼唤
于是他们饮这些水，尽管这里幽暗
　　　因为现在是黑夜。

我渴念这生生不息的源泉。

在这生命食粮中我清楚地看见它

　　　尽管现在是黑夜。

十二

像一个康复期病人，我抓住
码头上伸出的手，再次感到
一种异样的安慰，当我踏上陆地

发现那帮忙的手依然抓紧我的，
鱼一样冷，枯瘦，究竟是引领
还是被引领，我不确定

因为走在我身边的这位高个男人
好像是盲人，尽管在拐杖的帮助下
他挺直走着像一株灯芯草，眼睛直盯着前方。

于是我认出他本人
在汽车之间的柏油碎石路上，
冷硬尖锐像一丛黑刺李。

他的嗓音与百脉千川的元音一起旋转
重返我身边，尽管还没开口，
检察官似的声音，或歌手的，

狡黠，迷醉，模仿，确定

如钢笔尖的下笔，干净利落，
然后他突然用拐杖击打

垃圾篓，说道，"你的义务
并不因任何共同仪式而免除。
你必须做的必须独立完成

所以重返日常。最重要的是为了
写作的快乐而写作。培养工作欲望
想象其港湾就像你夜晚的手掌

在乳房的太阳黑子中梦想太阳。
你正在斋戒，头晕，危险。
从这里离开，别那么认真，

让别人去穿麻布披木灰。
放手，放飞，忘记。
你已听得够久。是时候击响你的琴键。"

仿佛我只身信步太空
周围无不是我熟悉的事物。
雨点吹打我的脸

我清醒过来。"老父亲，母之子，

斯蒂芬的日记*中有这样一刻
四月十三日，置于我的星辰

之间的启示——那则日记
一直是我耳中的某种密码，
一种新顿悟的短祷文，

圣漏斗节。"① "管他呢，"
他嘲笑道，"还有么？英语
属于我们。你是在拨弄死火，

对于你这把年纪就是浪费时间。
所谓属民不过是傻瓜的游戏，
幼稚，就像你的乡巴佬朝圣。

做体面的事，你失去的自己比你
赎回的更多。保持切线距离。
当他们把圆变宽，是时候

去独自畅游并让大自然充满

---

*"斯蒂芬的日记"，见乔伊斯《一个青年艺术家的肖像》结尾。
① 典出《一个青年艺术家的肖像》第五章。斯蒂芬对学监说出
"漏斗"（tundish）一词，学监并不懂，故暴露了他的无知与傲
慢。斯蒂芬因而摆脱了长久以来的自卑感。

你的频率你的调号，

回音探测，搜寻，摸索，诱惑，

茫茫黑暗海面上的幼鳗之光。"

阵雨突变暴雨，柏油路

蒸腾咝响。当他迅速走开

大雨围绕他挺直的步态松开帘幕。

第三部分：斯威尼重生*

*这部分诗歌为斯威尼发声，他是七世纪阿尔斯特的国王，被圣罗南诅咒，变成鸟人并流亡树上。我的《迷失的斯威尼》改写了这个爱尔兰传说，但我相信这些诠释无需故事原型的支撑也能存在。当然，很多内容的想象语境已远离中世纪早期的爱尔兰。

第一条批注

握紧笔杆
迈出第一步
从整齐的一行
进入边缘。

斯威尼重生

我搅拌湿沙并振作自己
为攀爬那陡峭的山岗，
我的脑袋像潮湿的麻线团
因浸湿而浓密，但正开始
松开。
　　　　另一种气息
从河上吹来，苦涩
如亚麻作坊里的晚风。
原来的树都不见了，
树篱纤若花体字母
而整个圈地都消失
在崎岖小路和尖脊房屋下。

而我在那儿，自己都难以置信，
在那些太渴望相信我和我的故事的
人群中，即使这碰巧是真的。

松　开

如果麻线团彻底松开
我手指甲下积聚的东西
是从床头采集的白石灰。

而我耳中积聚的东西
是他们删剪情色后无法推进的
闲谈，在灯光下被孵化，

将不得不被弃学
尽管从那儿往后一切
都将是学习。

于是麻线团松开并松松地开阔起来
向后穿过那些领域，它们曾向前
推进我去理解我该承担的一切。

在山毛榉中

我是被安放又被遗忘的哨岗。

在我下方，一边是水泥路。
另一边，阉牛的藏身处，
饮水地的气息与抚慰
那个中学毕业生在那里觅得平静
以便在翻起淤泥的臭味中抚摸自己。

而树本身是陌生也是安慰，
是树干也是石柱。那常春藤
用它乳牙状的叶边和纤纤叶尖
缠绕树的纹理：是树皮还是石艺？

我观看红砖烟囱逐层
竖起它的雄蕊，
以及上方修理工的荒诞举动
如大山衬托下的苍蝇。

我感到坦克的进军
始于年轮的中心，

后畏缩于他们在水泥路面
每个粉碎的钉痕中重振的强权，
还有反戴护目镜的飞行员进入视野
那么低，我能看见驾驶舱的铆钉。

我守旧的界限树。我的知识树。
我根深叶茂、飞羽柔软的空中哨岗。

第一个王国

皇家的路是牛径。

太后蹲在板凳上

把牛奶的竖琴弦

拨进一只木桶。

贵族们拄着沧桑的手杖

对牛群的腿臀指手画脚。

计量单位的估算靠的是

满马车、满推车和满桶。

时间是落后的熟记法，记住名姓和不幸，

歉收，火灾，不公的处置，

洪水、谋杀和流产中的死者。

而如果我对这一切的权利仅来自

他们的赞同，那它还有什么价值？

我忽冷忽热。

他们两面逢迎。

传宗接代依然是

他们的执著，同样

虔诚、苛刻、毫无尊严。

第一次飞行

更像是梦游而非痉挛
然而那时候，连时代
也在痉挛——

贯穿我们的纽带和绳结
裂开
沿纹路蔓延。

当我贴近卵石和浆果，
野蒜的味道，重新学习
霜冻的音效

以及林音的意义，
我映在田野上的影子
不过是个衍生物，

我的空位是借口
为了变换营地，演练
老一套的负债和背叛。

他们逐一来到树下

每个兜里都有一枚石子

为发出鸣啭并唤我回来

而我将在他们走后

从枝叶间跌撞着落下

我的栖息地被撞歪。

我深陷纠缠

直到他们宣布我

是以战场为食者

所以我征服了新的高空

在他们目力不及之处勘测

他们的山中篝火，他们的宴饮

与斋戒，从苏格兰征来的军队

一如既往，诡计多端的人们

变换他们富有韵律的吟唱

为抵挡疾风的猛攻

而我欢迎并将

全力以赴地攀升。

飘　游

领头鸟和信天翁
滑翔数日无需一次振翅
皆非我所能及。

我向往鲣鸟的袭击，
苍鹭心无旁骛的
专注。

在秃鼻鸦群的同志情谊中，
在群落心怀恶意的警惕中，
我感到自在。

我学会不信任
布谷的魅惑
和椋鸟的闲话，

忠于强悍的牛雀，
常常让我的智力
与小心眼的鹡鸰拉平

常常屈服于
对水鸡和恐慌的
长脚秧鸡的悲悯。

我过于相信离群之鸟，
高估了乌鸫的淡定
和喜鹊的传闻。

但当金翅雀或翠鸟撕裂
日常事物的面纱，
我的双翼就会嗡鸣并拉紧

我俯下身，笨拙
而饱满，
随时准备冲刺。

警　觉

从一开始我就是幸运的
也受到挑战，总是被打击
以便确保我不会长大后
太抱希望太过轻信——

我问自己到底能不能
到底该不该
拒绝服从，这时我听见
雌狐发情的狂吠。

她梳理欲望之网，
她挖出腐肉和闪电，
她打破矜持的
模范星辰的坚冰——

并让我扎根原地不动，
警觉，失望，
在我古老神秘的
前哥白尼夜空下。

教　士

我听见棚舍里传来
对牛说出的新祷文，在瓦罐和
隐蔽的蒸馏器上发现他的踪迹，

在清晨的第一缕炊烟中
嗅到他香炉里的气味。
然后他继续前进

穿过沟壑，测步选址，
把主教权杖深深插入
堡垒的炉膛。

如果他只是让他自己那些
尖下巴的女住持和吟咏者
在圈地附近挖洞播种，

说他的拉丁文和甜言蜜语，
把他的羊皮纸和密信
通过水路寄出也就罢了——

但是不，他通过
敷油和命令去镇压，
他必须抢占先机。

历史将它的旗帜插在
他的山墙和尖塔
却将我驱逐到

逃避和抱怨的边地。
或是我叛逃？
说句公道话，毕竟

他为我辟出一条路
通往如此辽阔而中立的王国
我的虚空得以随意统治。

隐 士

他在他的空地边缘巡行
取舍之刃不曾放过
一个情感的树墩

他就像犁铧
埋入土中为支撑整个
力场，从马颈

戴着辔头并高高拉紧的
侧面弧线到手腕手肘
牢牢抓紧的目标——

越是野蛮地拉与推，
那振奋就来得
越深刻越平静。

大 师

他栖于自身之中
像秃鼻乌鸦栖于无顶之塔。

为了靠近，我不得不
攀上荒废的城墙
不退转，也不能抬眼
去寻找他从隐居的一隅
投来的守望的目光。

他会审慎地展开
他的书，克制地
一次一页且毫无
神秘，不过是我们都曾
写在石板上的古老法理。
羊皮纸上的每个字母都牢牢
安于各自的方寸。
每条箴言都各就其位。

像采石工人的锤子和楔子
在顽强的服役中得到验证。

像你在源泉的慰藉中

倚靠的压顶石。

多么无力啊，当我爬下

墙上没有扶手的阶梯，

在上方的振翅声中听见

决心与勇毅。

抄 工

我向来不喜欢他们。
就算他们优秀，他们也任性
多刺，如同他们
用来提取墨汁的冬青。
而如果我从来不是他们的一员，
他们也就无权否认我的位置。

在缮写室的沉寂中
一颗黑珍珠在他们体内凝结
像羽毛笔管中风干的残墨。
在赞美文的页边
他们又抓又挠。
他们大吼大叫，如果天太黑
或者粉太多导致羊皮纸干燥
或太少导致纸太油。

在字母的屁股下
他们放牧短视的愤怒。
怨恨播种在大写字母
不再卷曲的蕨草脑袋中。

偶尔我会突然起身

相隔数里看到在我的缺席中

每个后背倾斜的连笔并感到

他们逐页针对我去完善自身。

让他们记住，对于他们嫉妒的艺术

这可是不小的贡献。

一个清醒的梦

当我匆匆把盐抛撒在
她的尾翼，天空的长踏板
轻而易举地将我托起
毫不费力，也没有越界和意外
引发的任何动静。
仿佛一个不觉入睡的人
开始怀疑日光的宁静。

在栗树里

树叶下的体温，雍容地
脱下并撩起

将身体摊开在日光下的水塘
一个五十多岁的女王，丢下

手包和耳环。她干吗要在意
那细腿多刺的，

这位年老结实的苏珊娜①，走进
没过腰腹的潭水，

她身上有的地方光滑洁白
有的地方圆滚滚？

而那小小的死亡之鸟

① 苏珊娜，圣经人物，"苏珊娜与长老"是文艺复兴时期颇受欧洲画家青睐的宗教题材。丁托莱托的《浴后的苏珊娜》是其中佼佼者。

在她华丽躯体的某处

不停尖叫？当然没有。
她深呼吸，搅动水藻。

斯威尼的归来

云朵会撕碎片刻

露出下方的绿岛，远处的

牛群，沉睡的铁轨——

而我想象她几乎从椅上滑落的

衣裳，遮挡曙光的窗帘，她眼睑的

闪烁和萌动。

然后当我栖于窗台

凝望我缺席的金库

我像一个在敌后冒险的侦察兵

在麦田里探出头

先看一眼，他的突破引起的悸动

在他体内久久不能平息：

窗帘卷起，一只手镯

躺在阳光中，丰腴的风信子

已开始泄密。

她去哪儿了？整洁

平坦的床铺另一边，我挣扎于

镜中自己狂野的影像。

冬 青

本该下雪却下了雨。
我们去采冬青时

沟渠积水，水深及膝
我们的手上都是刺

雨流进袖子。
本该有果实的

但我们带回家的小枝
却闪烁如碎玻璃。

现在我在这儿，房间里点缀着
红果实、蜡树叶的东西，

我几乎忘了衣衫湿透
或盼望下雪的感觉。

我伸手去拿一本书如一个怀疑者，
让它在我手边闪烁，

黑字的灌木，发光的盾墙，
锋利如冬青，如坚冰。

艺术家

我爱他愤怒的样子。
他对岩石的固执，他从
青苹果中胁迫实质。

他像狗一样狂吠
对着自己狂吠的形象。
他也恨自己
把工作当成唯一有用的事——
那种期待被感激或赞美的
庸俗心态，对他来说
意味着偷窃。

他的坚毅得以坚持并更坚定
因为他所做的是自己所知的。
他的额头像一个用力抛出的滚木球
飞掠未被涂画的空间
在苹果背后，在山峦背后。

旧圣像

为什么，当一切已结束，我还保留它们？

一个两臂交叉胸前的爱国者在一束光中：
牢房的铁窗和他被判刑的脸
是这幅小蚀刻画中仅有的亮点。

一幅石版画，积雪的山丘，非法牧师的
红法衣，红制服的英国兵艰难逼近
而守望员跑来像狐狸越过山口。

制造煽动言论的旧委会
束紧的拷花皮鞋和西装背心如此体面，
他们的传奇名字成为告密者的名单

供出者是个袖口洁净的人，后排左三，
比其他人都更显眼，
正策划一场行动，那既是他自己的刑具

也是他人的毁灭，他名字的节奏本身
就是一连串代价高昂的背叛记录
如今变得透明，且无法估算。

忆往昔 [1]

大弥撒书摊开

垂下真丝缎带

祖母绿、朱紫、水白。

我们不及物地列席，

忏悔、领受。动词

夺取我们。我们拜。

然后我们举目望向名词。

祭坛石乃黎明而圣体匣是正午，

红字一词本身便是布满血丝的落日。

如今我住在一处著名的海滨

那里的海鸟在凌晨啼鸣

如不信的魂灵

甚至那海滨大道的围墙

我倚靠它以确信

也很难诱使我相信。

---

① 原文为天主教弥撒中常用的拉丁文短语：In Illo Tempore。

在路上

前方的路
不断匀速
席卷而来，
路沿滴水。

在我手中
像来之不易的战利品，
是方向盘
空空的圆。

迷离的驾驶
让所有道路如一：
炽天使出没的托斯卡纳
乡间小路，多尔多涅

碧绿的橡树小径
或穿过麦田的小路
那个有钱的青年
在那里发问——

先生，我要做什么
才能得救？
或者那条路
那儿有只土红背

黑白尾的鸟
像燧石和黑玉的
拼花地板，
在我上方盘旋

并惠临。
变卖所有
济贫拔苦。
我一跃而起

像人的灵魂
从口中羽化
伴着男高音起伏的
黑色花体拉丁文。

我生来悲伤，
诺亚的鸽子，
惊惶的影子
穿过鹿径。

146

若我着陆

将经由一扇

朝东的小窗

我曾从那儿挤进，

借助迷信

攀越天宇，

把酒言欢

在教堂山墙。

我会整夜栖息

在流放的石板，

然后藏在墓园

墙壁的缝隙

那里，多少手掌

在铁石心肠的

花岗岩许愿墙

不断磨损。

跟随我。

我将迁徙

从高高的洞口

进入麦色、煦暖的峭壁，

沿着凹凸不平、

粘土地的通道，

拂面、拍翅，

抵达最深的洞室。

那里，一只饮水的鹿

被刻入岩石，

它的腰腿和脖颈

随着石头的轮廓起伏，

雕琢的线条

弯成一个紧张

企盼的口鼻

和一个张大的鼻孔

嗅探干涸的源头。

至于我的变化之书

我将冥想

面如岩石的守夜

直至那长期迷惘的

灵魂破壁而出

在枯竭的源泉

扬起尘埃。

山楂灯笼

1987

给伯纳德和简·麦凯布

河床，干涸，一半落满树叶。
我们，聆听树木间的河流。

目 录

155　致　谢　343

157　字母表　345

162　特米纳斯　348

164　来自写作的边界　350

166　山楂灯笼　351

167　石　磨　352

169　日光下的艺术　353

171　寓言岛　354

174　来自良心共和国　356

177　冰　雹　358

180　两则便笺　360

182　石头的判决　361

183　来自无言之地　362

185　死亡之舟　363

187　匙　饵　364

188　悼念罗伯特·菲茨杰拉德　365

189　往日球队　　　　　　　　366

190　空　地　　　　　　　　　367

199　牛奶工厂　　　　　　　　376

200　失去蕾切尔的夏天　　　　377

203　许愿树　　　　　　　　　379

204　一张来自冰岛的明信片　　380

205　孔雀翎　　　　　　　　　381

207　格罗图斯与柯文蒂娜　　　383

209　坚守航向　　　　　　　　384

211　子弹之歌　　　　　　　　385

214　沃尔夫·托恩　　　　　　387

216　拍摄脚本　　　　　　　　388

218　来自期待之乡　　　　　　389

221　淤泥异象　　　　　　　　391

224　消失的岛屿　　　　　　　393

225　筛　箩　　　　　　　　　394

致　谢

感谢以下编者，本集中的一些诗最初发表在这些报刊上：《田野》《学位袍》《哈泼斯杂志》《哈佛杂志》《诚实的阿尔斯特人》《欢迎来到爱尔兰》《爱尔兰时报》《伦敦书评》《歌》《犁铧》《诗歌簿协会增刊》《爱尔兰诗歌评论》《苏格兰人》《塞内加评论》《三便士评论》《泰晤士报文学增刊》《韵文》。

九首诗曾发表在《冰雹》（伽勒利出版社，1984）。《空地》的更早版本曾发表在限量版诗集，柯尔那莫纳出版社，1986年。《来自良心共和国》曾作为小册子出版，1985年人权日。《字母表》是写给哈佛大学优等生联谊会的诗，1984年。《寓言岛》写给威廉·戈尔丁，收录在《威廉·戈尔丁，其人其书：七十五岁诞辰献礼》（费伯，1986）；《消失的岛屿》最初在宴请蒂姆·塞弗林的晚餐上朗读，由圣布伦丹协会主办。

字母表

他父亲用交叠的手掌和手指
弄出一个影子，啃咬墙壁
像一个兔子头。他知道
上学后他会知道的更多。

在那里整整第一周他用粉笔画烟，
然后画分叉的树枝，人们称为 Y。
这是写字课。天鹅颈和天鹅背
形成 2，他现在能认也能说。

写字板上两根椽木和一条横木
是字母，有人读作 ah，有人读作 ay。
还有图表，还有标题，有正确的
握笔方式，也有错误的。

先是"抄写"，然后是"英语"
一把倾斜的小锄头代表正确。
墨水池的味道在教室的寂静中升腾。
窗前的地球仪倾斜像彩色的 O。

二

词形变化之歌飘在空中恍若和散那①
那是《基础拉丁语》第一册，
一列列单词栏如同石柱②，
带着大理石的纹理与威胁，浮现在他心中。

因为接着他在一所更严厉的学校受教育
这所学校以橡树林的守护圣人命名
在那里课程依据钟声的轰鸣而变换
他离开拉丁语论坛前往新书法的

树荫，仿佛回到家中。
这个字母表的字母是树木。
大写字母是盛开的果园，
手写线条像蜷缩在沟渠里的荆棘。

在她网纱的衣裳和赤裸的双脚里，
在她卷发的谐音和林音里，
诗人的梦像阳光将他悄悄占据
并潜入那些幽暗的树丛。

---

① 和散那（hosanna），赞美上帝之语。
② 原文 column 兼有"专栏"和"石柱"之意。

他学习这另一种书写。他是抄工，

在他白茫茫的原野驱赶一队翎笔。

他斗室的门前，乌鸫飞奔轻拍。

然后自我否定，斋戒，纯粹的冷。

规矩到了北方就变得更严格。

他伏案书写，重新再来。

基督的镰刀在低矮的灌木里。

字迹光秃秃、墨洛温。[①]

三

地球仪旋转。他站在木质的 O 里。

他暗引莎士比亚。他暗引格雷夫斯。

时间夷平了学校和学校的窗子。

打捆机吐出草捆如打印件，一捆捆

禾束堆如 λ 立在丰收季收割后的田野

每一个土豆坑的 Δ 脸

被轻轻拍平并塑形为防止霜冻。

都没了，唯有 Ω 始终

---

① 墨洛温王朝，大约在公元五〇〇至七〇〇年间统治高卢和德国。墨洛温艺术倾向于抽象风格，脱离现实。

守望每一扇门，幸运的马蹄铁。

然而形音字，回荡空中，至高无上

如君士坦丁见到的空中文字 **"凭此印记"**[①]

依然能对他发号施令；或那位魔法师[②]，

他会在他房子的穹顶悬挂

一幅彩色的世界地图

这样，每当他走到外面，

宇宙的图形和"不仅是孤立的事物"

就会映入他的眼底。一如从小小的舷窗

宇航员看到他所源自的一切，

那升起、晶莹、独特、光亮的 O

像一枚被放大的飘浮的卵——

或如我自己睁大的无思的眼睛

---

① 据说公元三一二年十月，君士坦丁大帝在出征米尔维安大桥
战役前，看到太阳上方有光的十字，旁边还有一句希腊文，"IN
HOC SIGNO VINCES"（In this sign you shall conquer，凭此印
记，汝必得胜）。他让人在士兵们的盾牌上画上十字标记，结
果米尔维安大桥战役大获全胜。
② 指意大利文艺复兴时期的学者马尔西里奥·费奇诺（Marsilio
Ficino，1433–1499），本来学医，后转向哲学和其他人文学科，
对魔法、占星术感兴趣，认为占星术有助于促进个人的内心生
活和宇宙之间的和谐。

好奇地注视梯子上的泥瓦匠

看他擦拭我们的山墙，用他的抹刀尖，

写下我们的名字，一个个奇怪的字母。

特米纳斯 ①

一

当我在那儿翻找，我会找到
一棵橡果和一枚生锈的螺钉。

若我抬起眼，一根工厂的烟囱
和一座休眠的山峰。

若我听，一个转轨的火车头
和一匹疾走的马。

有什么奇怪吗，若我认为
我也会改变想法？

二

当他们说起松鼠精明的窖藏
那就像圣诞节的礼物一样发光。

---

① 古罗马的界限之神。

162

当他们说起不义之财

我兜里的硬币就像烧红的炉盖。

我是分界渠也是分界渠的两堤

承受着双方所属的限极。

三

挑两个水桶比挑一个容易。

我成长在两者之间。

我的左手放上标准的铁砝码。

右手放入使天平倾斜的最后一颗谷粒。

男爵领地和教区在我的出生地相遇。

当我站在中央的踏脚石上

我是中流里马背上最后的伯爵

依然在谈判,在他同伴听力可及的范围内。

来自写作的边界

紧张与虚无弥漫那个空间
当车停在路上，军队检查
它的牌子和牌照，一个人把脸

凑近你的车窗，你看见更多人
在远处的山上，目光沿着
轻托的枪蓄意打量，置你于射程之内

而一切都是纯粹的审问
直到步枪示意，你移开
以戒备且毫不在乎的加速——

有点更空虚，有点被耗尽，
因为心中的颤抖，如同往常，
屈从，是的，而且温驯。

所以你继续驶向写作的边界
那里同样的事情又发生。三脚架上的枪；
巡警拿着他开关式的麦克风重复

你的数据，等待厉声喊出
放行；神枪手从上方瞄准你
如同阳光中的一只鹰。

然后突然间你通行，被传讯但也被释放，
仿佛你从一道瀑布的背后穿过
驶上柏油碎石路的黑流

经过装甲车，摆脱两边
站岗的士兵，他们像树影
流入又流出光亮的挡风玻璃。

山楂灯笼

冬日的山楂不合时宜地燃烧，
山楂树的小果实，给小人物的小灯笼，
对他们别无所求，只要其维持
那自尊的灯芯燃烧不灭，
无须以耀眼的光亮使他们暂时失明。

但有时当你的呼吸散在霜中
那弥漫的形状就像第欧根尼
提着灯笼，寻找一个正义者；
最后你在山楂背后接受审视，
那是他举在眼前的枝上灯笼，
你在紧实的果肉和果核面前退缩，
你希望那扎出血的刺证明你清白，
被啄食的醇熟打量你，然后移开。

石　磨

珀涅罗珀[①]在密谋的保障下工作。

无论她夜里拆掉什么

白天都会继续纺织。

我呢，五十年来打磨同样的石头

我拆掉的再也无法复原。

我就像镜前的黑暗不得回报。

我准备好让我的表面经受一切影响——

地图绘制员，版面复印员，所有刻线和上墨。

我负责晦涩，他们肠卜。

对于他们，每次都是新的开始和洁净的石板。

对于我，不过是兜了一圈

仿佛涟漪在无声中完满。

---

① 奥德修斯忠贞的妻子，出自荷马的《奥德赛》。在丈夫远征
特洛伊未归的岁月里，她为了拒绝求婚者，故意拖延纺织的
工作。

就这样。要纪念我。想象那些

剥去的矿石表层。在一堆

旧石版印刷品上练习体外射精。

日光下的艺术

给诺曼·麦凯格 [1]

在即将喝下毒药的那天

苏格拉底告诉朋友们他一直在写作：

把伊索寓言改为诗。

而这并非因为苏格拉底热爱智慧

并倡导经过审视的人生。

原因只是他做了一个梦。

恺撒，或尼禄或者君士坦丁

或莎士比亚笔下任何编号的君王

到头来都像水坝崩塌

原来的全景潜伏水下

不得不在死亡场景前重新涌起——

你能相信他们信以为真的梦。

但苏格拉底几乎不。直到，也就是，

---

[1] 诺曼·麦凯格（Norman MacCaig, 1910–1996），苏格兰诗人。"二战"期间曾作为"出于道义原因而拒服兵役者"入狱。

他告诉朋友们他一生中反复
出现的梦，重复同一个指示：

实践这门艺术，在那一刻之前
他一直以为这门艺术是哲学。
因此，有天赋的人有福了，

若从一开始就实践正确的艺术——
比如说，诗歌，或钓鱼，它们的夜晚无梦；
它们深沉的全景涌起又逝去

如日光穿过鱼竿和笔尖的眼。

寓言岛

一

尽管他们是被占领的国度
唯一的边界就是内陆
他们绝不屈服于任何人
坚信这个国家是一座岛屿。

在遥远的北方，有一个地区，
每个当地人都认为是"海滨"，
那里有一座山拥有不同的名字。

占领者把它称作玄武角。
太阳的墓碑，东部的农民说。
醉酒的西部人叫它孤儿的乳房。

旅行者要想知道他的方位
必须侧耳倾听——因为没有地图
标出他知道他已经越过的界线。

同时，骗人的当地人不断重复
那些他们假装不信的预言
预言说那座山底下有一个点

所有的名字都在那里汇合，

（有朝一日）他们将在那里开采真理的矿石。

二

起初，那里有一座钟楼

每天正午敲一声钟

以此纪念独眼的造物主。

至少，这是最初的想法

传教士抄工在土著传统里

发现它并记下。但即使如此

以后视的眼光，你不能确定

此中没有寓言的成分，

因为他们所有早期的手稿都充满

风格化的眼睛图形和反复出现的注释

那些古老的修正主义者根据

词根眼睛与陆地得出岛屿一词。①

---

① eye（眼睛）+land（陆地）=island（岛屿）。

三

如今，考古学家开始为那些注释做注。
一派认为，巨石圈是单纯的象征；
另一派认为是聚会点或茅屋的基石。

一派认为古老地板上的桩孔
首先代表虹膜上的瞳孔。
另一派认为桩孔就是桩孔。等等——

如同颠覆者与合谋者
总是怀着强烈的占有欲去竞争
讲述真正"岛国故事"的权利。

四

年长者梦见乘船旅行和港口
他们也有自己的故事，比如那个
卧病在床的人，至死依然坚信

开凿巴拿马运河
意味着海洋里的水都排空
岛屿将在扩张中消失。

来自良心共和国

一

当我降落在良心共和国
引擎熄火时，一片宁静，
我能听见杓鹬在跑道上空。

在边检站，工作人员是个老头
他从朴素的外衣取出钱夹
给我看了我爷爷的照片。

海关的女人要我说出
我们传统的偏方和护符用以
治疗哑默并转移恶毒目光。

没有脚夫。没有译员。没有出租车。
你背负你自己的负担，很快
你依仗特权的症状就消失了。

二

在那里雾是不祥之兆，但闪电

象征普遍的善，父母在雷雨中
把襁褓里的婴儿挂在树间。

盐是他们珍贵的矿藏。而海螺
在诞生与葬礼中被托到耳边。
一切墨汁与颜料的基础是海水。

他们神圣的象征是一条非写实的船。
船帆是一只耳朵，桅杆是倾斜的笔杆，
船体是嘴的形状，龙骨是睁开的眼睛。

在就职典礼上，人民领袖
必须宣誓拥护不成文的法令并哭泣
为自己傲慢追求公职而涤罪——

并声明他们坚信所有生命涌自
眼泪中的盐，那是天神的哭泣，
因为他梦见他的孤独绵绵无尽。

三

我从那俭朴的共和国回来
两手空空，海关的女人
坚称我自己就是我的免税品。

老头起身，注视我的脸
然后说经官方认证
我现在是双重国籍。

因此他希望我回到家后
以他们的代表自居
用我的母语为他们代言。

他们的使馆，他说，遍布各地
但都各自为政
没有任何大使能够发声。

冰 雹

一

我的脸颊被不断击打：
突如其来的冰雹
骤降并反弹在路上。

当天空再度放晴
那被鞭打的与可知的
已然撤退

留下我在那里碰运气。
我做了一个坚硬的小球
滚烫的水从我手中流出

就像我此刻
从那痛失的、融化的真实事物中
创造这首诗。

二

尽管如此，必须认真对待

那些冰雹的顽童。
他们怎样拒绝准许，

连续敲击教室的窗
像尺子打在手掌，
他们怎样最初完好

转瞬就变成肮脏的雪泥。
托马斯·特拉赫恩①拥有光明的麦子
作为证明和奇迹

但对于我们，那是冰雹的刺痛
和艾迪·戴蒙德②不被刺痛的手
在荨麻中觅食。

三

乳头与蜂房，咬肿，
这几乎令人快乐的小橡果
被预示又被否决

---

① 托马斯·特拉赫思（Thomas Traherne，1636 或 1637-1674），
十七世纪英国诗人。
② 希尼在当地的朋友。

当冰雹结束

而一切都在说等等。

等什么？等了四十年

才说那里，那里有关于

你结局的最真实预示——

在那膨胀中

当无声中云开日出

一辆汽车开着雨刷继续前行

在雪泥中留下完美的印迹。

两则便笺

一

我倔强的老朋友，你怎样伺机
发泄正当的愤怒！
谁能像你那样怂恿我

你要求灵魂诚实
正直像镀锌的水桶
并且会踢它来验证？

或将它夷平如地毯。
那么，当然，当你自我攻击，
你气势汹汹。

二

鲁莽、防刺并且孤独。
来自晚祷和道德挑战的
旧国度的劫掠者，

碰撞那些
你以为还在的屏障，
滑入稀薄的空气。

哦，正直与自我伤害的祈祷台
摇摇欲坠：
万福并永别。

石头的判决

当他站在审判席上，
手握拐杖，头上依然戴着宽檐帽，
他的伤害来自自我怀疑，来自
对甜言蜜语和借口的古老蔑视，
心不在焉地说出对他的判决是不公正的。
一生沉默寡言，他对他依赖的
终极法庭的期待超过言语。

就让它如同赫尔墨斯的审判，
石堆之神，石头乃判决
坚实地抛在他脚边，在他周围堆起
直到他站在使他超凡入圣的
齐腰深的石堆间：也许是门柱
或倒塌的围墙，那里猪草掩埋沉默，
终将被某个人打破，"这里
他的灵魂徘徊"，这已说得太多。

来自无言之地

我听说一个讲逻辑且健谈的国家
用一块白金当作他们
标准的度量单位，
王座厅和墓葬室都经过
各种严密的计算和预测。
在那金属的内核我会感到自在，
沉睡在一切体系的中心。

我们是流散的民族，我们的历史
是一种晦涩的忠诚。
何时，为何，我们开始流亡
沦为被语言压迫者，我们不知，
但团结如洪水在我们内心涌起
当听闻他们有关婴儿的传说，
讲述婴儿乘柳条船漂向命运
或国王的灵柩被举起、漂远
在河流之肩或远渡入海。

当我们认出自己的，我们步调一致
但也并非完全相同。

我最深切的接触在地下

背靠背悬在高峰期地铁的吊环上

还有一次在博物馆，我从

一个人的脖子和肩膀吸入春的应许，

那人假装沉浸于展览中

那沉默至极的磨石。

我们无言的假设具有

启示的力量。我们还能怎么知道

我们中究竟谁第一个

在丰饶的民主中寻求认可和选票，

谁又将是最后一个并杀死我们的语言？

与此同时，如果我们听见鱼跃

而没看到鱼，只见它的涟漪，

那意味着我们中又一个人正在某处垂死。

死亡之舟

希尔德大限来临时还是壮年，
他渡至彼岸进入神的看管。
他的士兵遵照他为丹麦人制定
法典时的吩嘱料理他的后事：
肩负他远涉大海的洪波，
敬重的首领，长久的领袖。
戴项圈的船首驶入海港，
船体覆冰，缆绳拉紧。
他们将心爱的主人平放船上，
在船中央，在桅杆下
安放这赐指环者。奇珍异宝
和昂贵戎装堆在他身上。
我此前从未听说过一艘船满载
如此精良的兵戈、刀剑
及铠甲。聚集的珍宝将他
覆盖：它们将持续远行
在波澜起伏的海上。
他们慷慨地装饰他的遗体
不亚于那些最初的哀悼者，
他们在他孩童时将他抛弃

让他孤身下水乘风破浪。

他们在他头顶上方竖起

一面金色旗帜，任由他

随着波涛漂流，哀哭他

且痛悼他们的损失。没人能说出，

宴厅里没有智者或沧桑的老兵

确知究竟谁打捞起那个负荷。

《贝奥武甫》，第 26-52 行

匙饵

所以一种新的比喻被赋予我们，
于是我们说：灵魂可被比作

孩童在铅笔盒滑盖下
发现的一枚匙饵，

仅此一瞥便足以想象一生，
升扬，自由，从乌有处绕回线轴——

一颗返回黑暗上空的流星。
逃离他同时燃烧他

如圣经中的富人坠入深渊时
苦苦哀求的一滴水。

然后离场，像锃亮的英雄头盔
在船中央，在急流上。

离场，或者，如光的玩具
钓起他逆流而上，什么都没抓住。

悼念罗伯特·菲茨杰拉德[①]

每一把斧头的托座就像方形

入口，通往史前巨石坟墓，

石板甬道不断敞向前方，

去面对又一道托臂石门，

然后又敞向另一道。没有最后的门，

唯有石槛，石柱，石梁

重复着进来，进来，进来，进来。

过梁与立柱在黑暗中飞逝。

在弓弦唱响燕子的音符后，

箭的迁徙是它的轨迹，

在每个托座留下轻柔的呼吸。

伟大的考验结束，羊肠弦依然低鸣，

这一次它的远行超出一切已知，

完美地趋向虚空的中心。

① 罗伯特·菲茨杰拉德（Robert Fitzgerald，1910–1985），美国诗人、批评家、翻译家。他翻译的古希腊史诗广泛流传。

往日球队

薄暮。苍穹。围栏更衣室

正式而朦胧，映在棕褐色

（永）夏的爱德华时代

阿尔斯特。可以是印度

或英格兰。或任何旧阅兵场

蓄胡子的承租人盛装走出

摆出交叉手臂的造型，肌肉发达，

忠贞不渝且永不服输。

默尤拉庄园足球俱乐部！卡斯尔道森①的儿子们！

锅炉工和亚麻工！外公麦凯恩！

团队精神，围墙里的庄园，亚麻作坊，

在你缺席时，成为历史

如那些轻轻鼓掌、重重撞击的足球竞技。

平稳的灵柩驶过平视的目光。

---

① 卡斯尔道森（Castledawson），希尼的出生地。

空 地

纪念 M.K.H.[①]，1911-1984

她教我她叔叔曾经教她的：
最大的煤块怎样轻易就裂开
如果你找对纹理和锤子的角度。

那放松而迷人的敲击声，
被接纳又被遗忘的回音，
教我敲打，教我放手，

教我在锤子与煤块之间
面对音乐。此刻又教我聆听，
发现那线性漆黑背后的富饶。

---

① 即 Margaret Kathleen Heaney，希尼的母亲。

一

一百年前抛出的小卵石
不断逼近我，第一枚石子
瞄准一位曾祖母背叛的额头。
小马受惊，暴乱开始。
她低低蹲在轻便马车里
冲出危险的人群，第一个礼拜天
她奔下悬崖去做弥撒。
他策马穿过小镇和"伦迪！"①的喊声。

叫她"改宗者"。"与异族通婚的新娘"。
不管怎样，这是我妈妈
这边继承的风俗画，
如今她走了，轮到我处置。
没有银饰和维多利亚蕾丝，
只有豁免和被豁免的石子。

---

① 伦迪（Robert Lundy，死于 1717 年），一六八八至一六八九年围
攻德里期间的军事指挥官，他的名字后被用来泛指叛徒。

二

擦亮的地板毡发光。黄铜水龙头发光。

那些瓷杯子很白很大——

包含糖碗糖罐的完好无损的套组。

水壶鸣叫。三明治和茶味司康饼

各就各位。为防止挥发，

黄油必须避开阳光。

不要掉面包屑。不要晃椅子。

不要去够。不要指。搅拌时不要弄出噪音。

那是新街 5 号，逝者之地，

外公从他的地方复活，

眼镜向后推到干净的光头上，

迎接一个迷惑的回家的女儿，

甚至在她敲门之前。"怎么了？怎么了？"

然后他们一起坐在发光的屋子里。

三

当其他人都去做弥撒，

我是她的全部，我们削土豆。

它们打破沉默，一个个跌落

像焊料滚下焊接的烙铁：

清冷的慰藉在我们之间，共享物

在一桶清水中闪闪发光。

然后再跌落。彼此的劳作激起

愉快的小水花，让我们回过神来。

所以当教区牧师在她床边

为临终者祈祷，锣鼓喧天，

一些人应和，一些哭泣，

我想起她的头曾俯向我的头，

她的呼吸在我的呼吸里，我们流畅的下刀——

我们一生中再没有那样靠近。

四

害怕刻意反而使她刻意

装作无能为力，每当碰到

"超出她能力"的发音。贝托尔特·布莱克^①。

每次她都设法发出受挫

而偏差的语音，仿佛掌握

一种词汇会让她背叛

那些受挫的与无力的。

挑战多过骄傲，她会告诉我，"你

什么都知道。"所以在她面前

我管辖我的舌头，一种真正

掌握且得力的背叛，

背叛我更熟知的事物。我会唯唯诺诺，

恰当地陷入错误语法

让我们结盟并保持独立。

---

① 即贝托尔特·布莱希特（1898–1956），德国诗人、戏剧家。
此处指母亲不标准的发音（Brek）。

五

刚从晾衣绳取下的床单阴凉

让我觉得里面想必还有潮气

但是当我握住麻布的两角

和她拉伸，先沿褶边纵向

再沿对角线，然后拍打、抖动

织物，仿佛横风中的船帆，

发出脱水的起伏的重音。

所以我们拉伸、折叠，最后手手相贴

仅一瞬间，仿佛什么都没发生，

因为没有什么不是此前日复一日

一直发生的，不过是一触即离，

后退是为了再度接近，

在移步中我是 x 她是 o[①]

铭刻在她用废弃的面口袋缝制的床单里。

[①] 一种井字格游戏。

六

在复活节最初的兴奋期，

圣周期间的种种仪式

是我们《儿子与情人》阶段的高潮。

子夜之火。复活节烛台。

肘贴肘，很高兴能在拥挤的教堂

前方并肩跪在一起，我们跟随经文

和仪式规则接受圣水盂的祝福。

如同母鹿向往溪水，我的灵魂亦然……

浸水。擦干。水被注入呼吸。

圣水与圣膏圣油混合。

盛器叮当。庄重的焚香，

自豪地领受赞美诗作者的呐喊：

日日夜夜我的泪水是我的面包。

七

在最后的时刻，他对她说的话
几乎比他们一生加起来还多。
"星期一晚上你将在新街，
我会来找你，当我走进门
你会很高兴……不是吗？"
他的头俯向她倚靠的头。
她听不见但我们都太欣喜。
他叫她乖女孩。然后她死了，
寻找脉搏的努力被放弃，
而我们在那里都确知一件事。
我们伫立环绕的那个空间被清空，
到我们内部去延续，它穿透
那些突然敞开的空地。
恸哭被砍伐，纯粹的变化已发生。

八

我想起不断环绕一个空间，

绝对空无，绝对之源，

那里，被装点的栗树失去它在

我们房前树篱与桂竹香上方的阵地。

白木屑跳来跳去，高高扬起，

我听见短斧错落有致的

精准砍伐，噼啪，听见

震颤的树梢及其全部的残骸

在茂育中叹息、轰然倒下。

曾经深植，久已消逝，我同龄的

种在果酱罐、埋在坑里的栗子树，

它的沉重与沉默今已成为明亮的缺席，

一个开枝散叶的灵魂，永远

沉默，在被聆听的沉默之外。

牛奶工厂

管道排出兔尾巴似的泡沫旋涡。
我们停在对岸观望
乳水从牛乳本身被刺穿的
一边流出，瓦罐中的物质溢出
漫过白色灵泊的地板，那里轮班工人
一刻不停地跋涉，工厂
保持它的距离，像一艘甲板明亮的星舰。

我们，如露水中眼神温柔的牛犊，
惊奇并融入荧光。

失去蕾切尔①的夏天

土豆田在盛放，

　　　　硬硬的青李挂在

你后门的李树上

　　　　每一丛有浆果的灌木

都闪闪发光且娇艳欲滴

　　　　每当倾盆大雨落在

被淹的干草和泛滥的沟渠。

　　　　月亮周围有一个环。

整个夏天都泡在水里

　　　　然而每个人都不愿

相信雨谄媚的方式

　　　　和成长的情绪

因为对夏天毫无保留的慷慨

　　　　所持的全部信心

---

① 希尼的侄女，弟弟休（Hugh）的女儿。

在上个五月崩溃，当我们为你装殓

　　　　一袭白衣，你苍白的脸

在事故中受伤，但平静，

　　　　如此绝对地平静，

而落日无情地坠落

　　　　而我们内心

每一个同情的音区渴望

　　　　将电影回放，

好让你踏上公路

　　　　踩着你明亮的单车，

和往常一样安全，

　　　　穿过，再沿小路骑行，

扭曲的辐条全都伸直，

　　　　可怕的刹车痕迹消失。

但不能。那么就让这倾盆大雨淹没

　　　　我们记忆的河床

直到，在滚滚水流中，

　　　　你也许可以走过的人生

梦幻地摇曳、拖动

　　宛若柔羽的水草

诱惑并平静我们的凝视

　　唤起我们的需要。

许愿树

我想象她是那棵死去的许愿树，
见它被拔起，连根带枝，升天，
那些曾随着一个又一个又一个

需求钉入它强壮树干和树皮的东西
坠落如雨：硬币，徽章，铁钉，
倾泻而下仿佛彗星的尾巴，

新铸又消散。我看见一个幻象：
一个空灵的树枝头冠从水汽腾腾的云朵后升起
一张张仰望的脸在许愿树曾站立的地方聚集。

一张来自冰岛的明信片

当我伸手去试探温泉几码外的
小溪，我什么也听不见
除了所有咕哝沸腾的淤泥。

然后我身后的向导说，
"微温①。我想你大概想知道
luk 在古冰岛语里是手的意思。"

你也会想知道（但你已知晓）
当水的掌心找到我的手掌
那微漾和压力是多么寻常。

_____

① lukewarm。

孔雀翎

给黛西·加奈特

六天前圣水倾泻而下

为你施洗命名，施展它的魔法，

擦干你的石板，我们希望，到永远。

但如今你的生活就是睡觉和吃饭，

再加上爱的轻抚，足以

满足你的需求，黛西，黛西，英国侄女。

格洛斯特郡：它的景色呈现

在我眼前是树林和雾岚，

我的风景，如同你母亲的，

不同于这柔美成熟的景色：

园林、草地和砖头，

私有，幽居，围墙，怀旧。

我来自贫瘠的农场和湿地，

那是古老的杂色拼布，历史的掷币

游戏使之凌乱不堪。

但这里，为了你，我改变

我马道的嗓音为花园的音色，

用科茨沃尔德的石子铺筑沼泽。

缕缕缠绕的家庭纽带交叠

为双心一体的同心结。

未来不是我们的。我们将编就

一座姻亲的迷宫，将点头挥手，

信任但并不亲密——

所以这封情书要告诉你

一个温暖的七月，你躺在

布莱德利受洗、微笑，

而我，你碧绿庭院的宾客，

正坐在西窗下写作，

自觉于渐浓的幽暗。

我宛若置身库尔庄园。

那么，在我离开你庄严的家园之前，

让我们祈祷。愿沃土与耕田，

随凯尔特和撒克逊的血液变深，

哺育你去热爱家园和树林——

在这里，临别前我为你写下这首诗，

如同草地上的孔雀翎。

（1972）

格罗图斯与柯文蒂娜①

远离家乡，格罗图斯将祭坛献给柯文蒂娜，

她的右手握着一株水草，

左手持水罐，溢出一条河。

无论在哪儿，只要格罗图斯看一看流水，他就如在家园；

而当他忆起刻有他名字的石头，

他胸骨下的枯竭河道便开始

汹涌并变暗——多少有点类似

想起他的矮祭坛对我产生的影响。

还记得吗，当我们的电水泵崩溃，

我们给它注入一桶桶水，傻瓜般愤怒

并畏畏缩缩打电话给隔壁农舍

恳请有人前来修理它？

而当它又开始砰砰运转，

欢庆龙头的满满力量和水喷涌的

纯粹事实，你怎样感到你永远不会

---

① 柯文蒂娜（Coventina），古代凯尔特女河神。在英国乡间河流发源处常有她的祭台。希尼在其中一个祭台上发现"格罗图斯"（Grotus）的名字，这是罗马人的常用名。罗马人曾占领英国数百年。此诗作于希尼夫妇拜访哈德良长城后。

浪费一滴水，永远更懂得它的价值。

你是否觉得我们可以重演一遍？

我将是格罗图斯，你是柯文蒂娜。

坚守航向

螺旋桨在水下，船舱轰鸣，灯光——
不被留意但每晚都坚守在那里，
大渡轮思索它们的航程。
我嫉妒你今早看到的船景，
入港，笨重，倾斜的烟囱。

景色高远空旷，你站在
我们阁楼窗前。迢遥的托莱多蓝调。
而你身后的书架上
我们从科瓦东加带回的阿尔卑斯蓟
垂下它多刺的花冠。

去年秋天我们焖燃烘烤
如那些在上方守夜的尖塔
或如格伦德尔的铁爪
抓住宴饮厅的屋顶。然后我们突破
或熬过。这本身就是酬报。

我们是次日清晨的纵欲者。
当鸥鸟在深邃的海峡上空啼鸣

你伫立，伫立，拨弄头发，

想象我是你闺房里的麦克惠尔 ①，

直心肠，一根筋，不懂耍花招。

---

① 麦克惠尔（MacWhirr），康拉德作品《台风》里的船长，性格
刻板。

子弹之歌

我在院子里久久凝望

　　　　如常的星辰，寂静

而迷人的行星，灯笼般明亮

　　　　挂在我们漆黑山丘的上空。

然后有颗星在动，我觉得，

　　　　因为确实有某种东西

以炽烈而无声的速度

　　　　从拥挤的天际线后上移

当它触及穹顶，横穿

　　　　另一星体弧形的轨迹

它飞升的样子就像

　　　　镰刀的锋刃穿过刈草。

"夜晚的天空里满是我们"，

　　　　一颗开始歌唱，

"我们的铅弹冰冷致命，

　　　　我们的轨迹翱翔。

我们的弹壳和驽钝的残片
　　　　在下方集结，
而正义惶恐地驻足旁观
　　　　如太阳映照北极雪。

我们的罪过偶然。指责，
　　　　指责，因为你必须。
那么，指责小伙子的精液或
　　　　指责月亮的月尘。"

当反弹的颤音逼近
　　　　然后在风中消逝，
那艰难的女低音飞掠，
　　　　星际的静谧统治

直到另一个火球发声：
　　　　"我们有铁的意志。
我们箍紧世事的体系
　　　　超越猎手和猎物。

橄榄山上的八福，
　　　　灵魂终止的欲念
都不能战胜我们
　　　　我们居于大理石的火焰

来自每一个平稳的目光

      眯缝，瞄准，停顿：

我们开火并釉涂事物的形状

      直到万物定型。"

现在风正吹过院落。

      云掩盖星辰。寂静

而迷人的行星消失

      在我们漆黑山丘的上空。

沃尔夫·托恩 [①]

轻盈如一叶小舟，机灵
却被诡计战胜，

我刻意佩戴肩章和帽徽，
书写有教养的文风，不为

我谋求的团结所动，
用一把剃刀扮演古罗马人。

我是扛在肩上的桨，到头来
却远离历险的大海和气息。

像抓挠柱或十字路口的旗杆，
不自在地置身于小农场主之间——

我曾被海底传来的
男人们的喊声唤醒，

——————
①沃尔夫·托恩（Wolfe Tone，1763–1798），爱尔兰革命领袖。

穿衬衣的男人们从深水中浮起，

当大西洋击碎我们船舱舷窗的遮光板，

大舰队分裂，爱尔兰缩小，

我们在光秃的桅杆下望风而逃。

拍摄脚本

他们骑车离开可能的过去
前往不可能的将来，手持镜头：
骑单车的教师，致敬讲母语者，
踏着一九二○年代如同未来。

镜头尽头依然踏车前行，
不去哪里也不离开。
紫红色调，"追随语言"。
漫长无声的连续镜头。全景并淡出。

然后是画外音，不同的爱尔兰语，
议论翻译工作和翻译一行的价格；
如草地里十九世纪的里程碑，
R.M. 巴兰坦①等名字浮现。

猫眼道钉的特写
向后拉伸为广角，法衣披肩，
教士帽，罗马领，喉结。

———————————
① 巴兰坦（R.M.Ballantyne，1825–1894），苏格兰儿童文学作家，代表作有《珊瑚岛》等。

定格他茫然的脸。播放剧组名单

而就在看似剧终时——
跟踪拍摄海滨的巨浪
冲向一根持续书写的棍棒，
将古老的字词写入流沙。

来自期待之乡

一

我们深居在祈愿语气之乡，
在听天由命的高高积云下。
我们有生之年不会这句话里有失落的窘窄，
我们祈求惠赐或恩准时崩溃的心态
勇气可嘉，足以度日。

一年一度我们聚集在欢庆场所，
那里孩子们在舞台和帐篷中
用古老的语言唱熟记的歌。
一位曾在兄弟会战斗过的拍卖商
历数种种我们永远以为
理当承受的屈辱，但即便他，
我觉得，也没有因此而采取行动。
铁口的扩音器震撼空气
但没人觉得自己该负责。他使我们坚定。
当我们反叛的国歌奏响，会议结束，
我们转身回家，在关卡前接受
加班民兵一如既往的骚扰。

二

接着，突然间，语气转变。
新通电的厨房里书本打开。
原本可能枕着奶牛腰瞌睡
一生的孩子们正忙着
在指定教材上用铅笔铺筑
他们最初的堤道。接下来
是四方的铺路石和祈使句，
充满需求的新时代。
他们会永久驱逐条件句，
这代人生来就对我们发自内心深处的
呐喊中的胜利无动于衷。
我们以隐忍取胜的信念
他们诅咒，聪明有加，
粗鲁无礼，如同撬棍。

三

看似最强大的已过期限。
未来在于底层的支持。
当我们居于秘密赞助人、
被动态守护天使的庇护下，

这些事物曾使我们强大，

如今却把威吓的利齿咬进我肩。

我对自己重复"击中"一词

并脱帽站在古铜色雷电

愈磨愈利的积云之下。

我渴望铁锤击在层叠的船板，

被操纵的桨架发出毫不妥协的回音，

好知道我们中总有一人从不偏离

直觉告诉他的正确行动，

并在陈述句中坚持立场，

暴雨来临时，他的船高扬。

淤泥异象

心脏暴露、头戴铁丝荆棘冠的雕像
依然在神龛屹立，野兔在喷气机
打盹的肚皮下跳跃，我们的程序员
和喷雾气的朋克迷在各自的岗位
出类拔萃。卫星连线传送的
主教祝福在我们上空飘扬，直升机场
为巡演的偶像和担架上的伤员维系
魔法保护下的圆圈。我们梦游
在惊惶与程式之间，为我们
最初的本土模特和最后的哑剧演员试镜，
从一定距离观察自己，占据高处
并保持轻松，如跳板上的男人
不断热身因为他不会跳水。

然后在多雾的中原，它显现，
我们的淤泥异象，仿佛一面淤泥的玫瑰窗
从闪光的潮湿中发明了自己，
一个蛛丝的轮，与它星云般的尘埃
轮毂同心，污浊而光辉。
我们听说过太阳静止和太阳

变换颜色，但我们被赐予
原初的泥土，改观且飞旋。
然后日落幽暗晦昧，雨刷
永远无法彻底擦净挡风玻璃，
水库有泥沙的味道，薄薄的绒毛
在头发和睫毛上积聚，有人
喜欢在额头抹一道污迹
为可能发生的情况做好准备。守夜
开始在积水的裂隙周围持续，
祭坛上香蒲驱逐了百合，
一群群伤员轮流来去
在租来的含淋浴的床位上。

见过神迹的一代人啊！
那些夜晚我们站在赭色露水里闻
马鞭草的霉味，或在枕上淡淡的
犁沟气息中醒来，当大家都在
谈论谁见过它，我们的恐惧
染上秘密的得意，只有我们自己
能胜任我们的生命。当彩虹
弯曲洪水的棕黄，横贯如河鼠背，
以至硬路肩上的司机们停下观看，
我们祈愿它消失，但也设想它是考验
将证明我们超出预期的价值。

当然，我们终于懂得那想法多蠢。

有一天它消失了，东面的山墙，

它战栗的花冠曾站稳的地方，

再度成为赤裸的废墟，蒲公英

在窗台上高高飘扬，苔藓

继续在蔓延中沉睡。照相机

从各个角度扫射此地，专家们

开始他们事后的阔论，我们所有人

挤在一起等待宏大阐释。

就那样，我们忘了那异象属于我们，

是我们唯一的机遇，去认识超凡

并跃入未来。可能的本源

被我们消耗于新闻。澄清之地

既没找回我们也没找回它自己——除了

你可以说我们幸存下来。那就说吧，看我们

曾有机会成为泥人，自信而疏离，

示现在我们自己眼中并示与世人。

消失的岛屿

曾经我们以为能永远扎根于
它的青山和无沙的海岸之间
在祈祷和守夜中度过绝望的夜晚。

曾经我们收集浮木，生起炉火
架起我们的大锅宛若苍穹，
岛屿在我们下面崩塌如浪波。

支撑我们的陆地仿佛只有
在绝境中拥抱它时才坚定。
我相信那里发生的一切都是幻景。

筛 箩

你从未见它被使用但依然能听见
筛箩上积聚的物料过滤并落下，

泥团与叶芽悄悄争论，
筛落的物料在下方堆积。

附着的，落下的，哪个更好？
抑或选择本身创造价值？

腿叉开，手灵活，开始一场哑剧，
为从想象中滤出事物的意义

好知道那个用筛箩提水的男人
他的故事中究竟发生了什么。

是有罪的无知，还是通过
筛滤与失落达成的否定之路？

希尼在北爱尔兰德里郡贝拉希村附近的泥炭地，
一九八七年（Bobbie Hanvey 摄）

Station Island

For Brian Friel

Contents

PART ONE

237   The Underground

238   La Toilette

239   Sloe Gin

240   Away from It All

242   Chekhov on Sakhalin

243   Sandstone Keepsake

244   Shelf Life

244   1. *Granite Chip*

244   2. *Old Smoothing Iron*

245   3. *Old Pewter*

246   4. *Iron Spike*

247   5. *Stone from Delphi*

247   6. *A Snowshoe*

248   A Migration

251   Last Look

253   Remembering Malibu

255   Making Strange

256   The Birthplace

258   Changes

259   An Ulster Twilight

261   A Bat on the Road

262   A Hazel Stick for Catherine Ann

263   A Kite for Michael and Christopher

264   The Railway Children

265   Sweetpea

266   An Aisling in the Burren

267   Widgeon

268   Sheelagh na Gig

270   The Loaning

272   The Sandpit

272   1. *1946*

272   2. *The Demobbed Bricklayer*

273   3. *The Sand Boom*

274   4. *What the Brick Keeps*

275   The King of the Ditchbacks

PART TWO: STATION ISLAND

281   Station Island

PART THREE: SWEENEY REDIVIVUS

311   The First Gloss

312   Sweeney Redivivus

313   Unwinding

314   In the Beech

315   The First Kingdom

316   The First Flight

318   Drifting Off

319   Alerted

320   The Cleric

321   The Hermit

322   The Master

323   The Scribes

324   A Waking Dream

325   In the Chestnut Tree

326   Sweeney's Returns

327   Holly

328   An Artist

329   The Old Icons

330   In Illo Tempore

331   On the Road

334   *Notes*

PART ONE

The Underground

There we were in the vaulted tunnel running,
You in your going-away coat speeding ahead
And me, me then like a fleet god gaining
Upon you before you turned to a reed

Or some new white flower japped with crimson
As the coat flapped wild and button after button
Sprang off and fell in a trail
Between the Underground and the Albert Hall.

Honeymooning, moonlighting, late for the Proms,
Our echoes die in that corridor and now
I come as Hansel came on the moonlit stones
Retracing the path back, lifting the buttons

To end up in a draughty lamplit station
After the trains have gone, the wet track
Bared and tensed as I am, all attention
For your step following and damned if I look back.

La Toilette

The white towelling bathrobe
ungirdled, the hair still wet,
first coldness of the underbreast
like a ciborium in the palm.

*Our bodies are the temples
of the Holy Ghost.* Remember?
And the little, fitted, deep-slit drapes
on and off the holy vessels

regularly? And the chasuble
so deftly hoisted? But vest yourself
in the word you taught me
and the stuff I love: slub silk.

Sloe Gin

The clear weather of juniper
darkened into winter.
She fed gin to sloes
and sealed the glass container.

When I unscrewed it
I smelled the disturbed
tart stillness of a bush
rising through the pantry.

When I poured it
it had a cutting edge
and flamed
like Betelgeuse.

I drink to you
in smoke-mirled, blue-black,
polished sloes, bitter
and dependable.

Away from It All

A cold steel fork
pried the tank water
and forked up a lobster:
articulated twigs, a rainy stone
the colour of sunk munitions.

In full view of the strand,
the sea wind spitting on the big window,
we plunged and reddened it,
then sat for hours in conclave
over the last of the claws.

It was twilight, twilight, twilight
as the questions hopped and rooted.
It was oarsmen's backs and oars
hauled against and lifting.
And more power to us, my friend,

hard at it over the dregs,
laying in in earnest
as the sea darkens
and whitens and darkens
and quotations start to rise

like rehearsed alibis:
I was stretched between contemplation
of a motionless point
and the command to participate
actively in history.

'*Actively?* What do you mean?'
The light at the rim of the sea
is rendered down to a fine
graduation, somewhere between

balance and inanition.

And I still cannot clear my head
of lives in their element
on the cobbled floor of that tank
and the hampered one, out of water,
fortified and bewildered.

Chekhov on Sakhalin

for Derek Mahon

So, he would pay his 'debt to medicine'.
But first he drank cognac by the ocean
With his back to all he travelled north to face.
His head was swimming free as the troikas

Of Tyumin, he looked down from the rail
Of his thirty years and saw a mile
Into himself as if he were clear water:
Lake Baikhal from the deckrail of the steamer.

That far north, Siberia was south.
Should it have been an ulcer in the mouth,
The cognac that the Moscow literati
Packed off with him to a penal colony –

Him, born, you may say, under the counter?
At least that meant he knew its worth. No cantor
In full throat by the iconostasis
Got holier joy than he got from that glass

That shone and warmed like diamonds warming
On some pert young cleavage in a salon,
Inviolable and affronting.
He felt the glass go cold in the midnight sun.

When he staggered up and smashed it on the stones
It rang as clearly as the convicts' chains
That haunted him. In the months to come
It rang on like the burden of his freedom

To try for the right tone – not tract, not thesis –
And walk away from floggings. He who thought to squeeze
His slave's blood out and waken the free man
Shadowed a convict guide through Sakhalin.

Sandstone Keepsake

It is a kind of chalky russet
solidified gourd, sedimentary
and so reliably dense and bricky
I often clasp it and throw it from hand to hand.

It was ruddier, with an underwater
hint of contusion, when I lifted it,
wading a shingle beach on Inishowen.
Across the estuary light after light

came on silently round the perimeter
of the camp. A stone from Phlegethon,
bloodied on the bed of hell's hot river?
Evening frost and the salt water

made my hand smoke, as if I'd plucked the heart
that damned Guy de Montfort to the boiling flood –
but not really, though I remembered
his victim's heart in its casket, long venerated.

Anyhow, there I was with the wet red stone
in my hand, staring across at the watch-towers
from my free state of image and allusion,
swooped on, then dropped by trained binoculars:

a silhouette not worth bothering about,
out for the evening in scarf and waders
and not about to set times wrong or right,
stooping along, one of the venerators.

Shelf Life

1. *Granite Chip*

Houndstooth stone. Aberdeen of the mind.

Saying *An union in the cup I'll throw*
I have hurt my hand, pressing it hard around
this bit hammered off Joyce's Martello
Tower, this flecked insoluble brilliant

I keep but feel little in common with –
a kind of stone age circumcising knife,
a Calvin edge in my complaisant pith.
Granite is jaggy, salty, punitive

and exacting. *Come to me*, it says
*all you who labour and are burdened, I
will not refresh you.* And it adds, *Seize
the day.* And, *You can take me or leave me.*

2. *Old Smoothing Iron*

Often I watched her lift it
from where its compact wedge
rode the back of the stove
like a tug at anchor.

To test its heat by ear
she spat in its iron face
or held it up next her cheek
to divine the stored danger.

Soft thumps on the ironing board.

Her dimpled angled elbow
and intent stoop
as she aimed the smoothing iron

like a plane into linen,
like the resentment of women.
To work, her dumb lunge says,
is to move a certain mass

through a certain distance,
is to pull your weight and feel
exact and equal to it.
Feel dragged upon. And buoyant.

3. *Old Pewter*

Not the age of silver, more a slither
of illiteracy under rafters:
a dented hand-me-down old smoky plate
full of blizzards, sullied and temperate.

I love unshowy pewter, my soft option
when it comes to the metals – next to solder
that weeps at the touch of a hot iron;
doleful and placid as a gloss-barked alder

reflected in the nebulous lid of a pool
where they thought I had drowned one winter day
a stone's throw from the house, when the whole
country was mist and I hid deliberately.

Glimmerings are what the soul's composed of.
Fogged-up challenges, far conscience-glitters
and hang-dog, half-truth earnests of true love.
And a whole late-flooding thaw of ancestors.

4. *Iron Spike*

So like a harrow pin
I hear harness creaks and the click
of stones in a ploughed-up field.
But it was the age of steam

at Eagle Pond, New Hampshire,
when this rusted spike I found there
was aimed and driven in
to fix a cog on the line.

What guarantees things keeping
if a railway can be lifted
like a long briar out of ditch growth?
I felt I had come on myself

in the grassy silent path
where I drew the iron like a thorn
or a word I had thought my own
out of a stranger's mouth.

And the sledge-head that sank it
with a last opaque report
deep into the creosoted
sleeper, where is that?

And the sweat-cured haft?
Ask the ones on the buggy,
inaudible and upright
and sped along without shadows.

5. *Stone from Delphi*

To be carried back to the shrine some dawn
when the sea spreads its far sun-crops to the south
and I make a morning offering again:
that I may escape the miasma of spilled blood,
govern the tongue, fear hybris, fear the god
until he speaks in my untrammelled mouth.

6. *A Snowshoe*

The loop of a snowshoe hangs on a wall
in my head, in a room that is drift-still:
it is like a brushed longhand character,
a hieroglyph for all the realms of whisper.

It was to follow the snow goose of a word
I left the room after an amorous blizzard
and climbed up attic stairs like a somnambulist,
furred and warm-blooded, scuffling the snow-crust.

Then I sat there writing, imagining in silence
sounds like love sounds after long abstinence,
eager and absorbed and capable
under the sign of a snowshoe on a wall.

The loop of the snowshoe, like an old-time kite,
lifts away in a wind and is lost to sight.
Now I sit blank as gradual morning brightens
its distancing, inviolate expanse.

A Migration

About a mile above
and beyond our place,
in a house with a leaking roof
and cracked dormer windows
Brigid came to live
with her mother and sisters.

So for months after that
she slept in a crowded bed
under the branch-whipped slates,
bewildered night after night
by starts of womanhood,
and a dream troubled her head

of a ship's passenger lounge
where empty bottles rolled
at every slow plunge
and lift, a weeping child
kept weeping, and a strange
flowing black taxi pulled

into a bombed station.
She would waken to the smell
of baby clothes and children
who snuggled tight, and the small
dormer with no curtain
beginning to go pale.

Windfalls lay at my feet
those days, clandestine winds
stirred in our lyric wood:
restive, quick and silent
the deer of poetry stood
in pools of lucent sound

ready to scare,
as morning and afternoon
Brigid and her sisters
came jangling along, down
the steep hill for water,
and laboured up again.

Familiars! A trail
of spillings in the dust,
unsteady white enamel
buckets looming. Their ghosts,
like their names, called from the hill
to 'Hurry', hurry past,

a spill of syllables.
I knew the story then.
Ferry Glasgow-Belfast,
then to the Dublin train
with their cases and boxes,
pram and cassette machine,

and then they miss the bus,
their last Wicklow connection –
the young ones scared and cross
in the lit bus station,
the mother at a loss.
And so in desperation

they start out for the suburbs
and into the small hours.
How it sweetens and disturbs
as they make their homesick tour,
a moonlight flit, street arabs,
the mother and her daughters

walking south through the land
past neon garages,

night lights haloed on blinds,
padlocked entries, bridges
swelling over a kind
mutter of streams, then trees

start filling the sky
and the estates thin out,
lamps are spaced more widely
until a cold moonlight
shows Wicklow's mountainy
black skyline, and they sit.

They change the cassette
but now the battery's gone.
They cannot raise a note.
When the first drops of rain
spit in the dark, Brigid
gets up and says, 'Come on.'

Last Look

in memoriam E.G.

We came upon him, stilled
and oblivious,
gazing into a field
of blossoming potatoes,
his trouser bottoms wet
and flecked with grass seed.
Crowned blunt-headed weeds
that flourished in the verge
flailed against our car
but he seemed not to hear
in his long watchfulness
by the clifftop fuchsias.

He paid no heed that day,
no more than if he were
sheep's wool on barbed wire
or an old lock of hay
combed from a passing load
by a bush in the roadside.

He was back in his twenties,
travelling Donegal
in the grocery cart
of *Gallagher and Son,*
Merchant, Publican,
Retail and Import.
Flourbags, nosebags, buckets
of water for the horse
in every whitewashed yard.
Drama between hedges
if he met a Model Ford.

If Niamh had ridden up
to make the wide strand sweet

with inviting Irish,
weaving among hoofbeats
and hoofmarks on the wet
dazzle and blaze,
I think not even she
could have drawn him out
from the covert of his gaze.

Remembering Malibu

for Brian Moore

The Pacific at your door was wilder and colder
than my notion of the Pacific

and that was perfect, for I would have rotted
beside the luke-warm ocean I imagined.

Yet no way was its cold ascetic
as our monk-fished, snowed-into Atlantic;

no beehive hut for you
on the abstract sands of Malibu –

it was early Mondrian and his dunes
misting towards the ideal forms

though the wind and sea neighed loud
as wind and sea noise amplified.

I was there in the flesh
where I'd imagined I might be

and underwent the bluster of the day:
but why would it not come home to me?

Atlantic storms have flensed the cells
on the Great Skellig, the steps cut in the rock

I never climbed
between the graveyard and the boatslip

are welted solid to my instep.
But to rear and kick and cast that shoe –

beside that other western sea
far from the Skelligs, and far, far

from the suck of puddled, wintry ground,
our footsteps filled with blowing sand.

Making Strange

I stood between them,
the one with his travelled intelligence
and tawny containment,
his speech like the twang of a bowstring,

and another, unshorn and bewildered
in the tubs of his wellingtons,
smiling at me for help,
faced with this stranger I'd brought him.

Then a cunning middle voice
came out of the field across the road
saying, 'Be adept and be dialect,
tell of this wind coming past the zinc hut,

call me sweetbriar after the rain
or snowberries cooled in the fog.
But love the cut of this travelled one
and call me also the cornfield of Boaz.

Go beyond what's reliable
in all that keeps pleading and pleading,
these eyes and puddles and stones,
and recollect how bold you were

when I visited you first
with departures you cannot go back on.'
A chaffinch flicked from an ash and next thing
I found myself driving the stranger

through my own country, adept
at dialect, reciting my pride
in all that I knew, that began to make strange
at that same recitation.

The Birthplace

I

The deal table where he wrote, so small and plain,
the single bed a dream of discipline.
And a flagged kitchen downstairs, its mote-slants

of thick light: the unperturbed, reliable
ghost life he carried, with no need to invent.
And high trees round the house, breathed upon

day and night by winds as slow as a cart
coming late from market, or the stir
a fiddle could make in his reluctant heart.

II

That day, we were like one
of his troubled pairs, speechless
until he spoke for them,

haunters of silence at noon
in a deep lane that was sexual
with ferns and butterflies,

scared at our hurt,
throat-sick, heat-struck, driven
into the damp-floored wood

where we made an episode
of ourselves, unforgettable,
unmentionable,

and broke out again like cattle
through bushes, wet and raised,
only yards from the house.

III

Everywhere being nowhere,
who can prove
one place more than another?

We come back emptied,
to nourish and resist
the words of coming to rest:

birthplace, roofbeam, whitewash,
flagstone, hearth,
like unstacked iron weights

afloat among galaxies.
Still, was it thirty years ago
I read until first light

for the first time, to finish
The Return of the Native?
The corncrake in the aftergrass

verified himself, and I heard
roosters and dogs, the very same
as if he had written them.

Changes

As you came with me in silence
to the pump in the long grass

I heard much that you could not hear:
the bite of the spade that sank it,

the slithering and grumble
as the mason mixed his mortar,

and women coming with white buckets
like flashes on their ruffled wings.

The cast-iron rims of the lid
clinked as I uncovered it,

something stirred in its mouth.
I had a bird's eye view of a bird,

finch-green, speckly white,
nesting on dry leaves, flattened, still,

suffering the light.
So I roofed the citadel

as gently as I could, and told you
and you gently unroofed it

but where was the bird now?
There was a single egg, pebbly white,

and in the rusted bend of the spout
tail feathers splayed and sat tight.

So tender, I said, 'Remember this.
It will be good for you to retrace this path

when you have grown away and stand at last
at the very centre of the empty city.'

An Ulster Twilight

The bare bulb, a scatter of nails,
Shelved timber, glinting chisels:
In a shed of corrugated iron
Eric Dawson stoops to his plane

At five o'clock on a Christmas Eve.
Carpenter's pencil next, the spoke-shave,
Fretsaw, auger, rasp and awl,
A rub with a rag of linseed oil.

A mile away it was taking shape,
The hulk of a toy battleship,
As waterbuckets iced and frost
Hardened the quiet on roof and post.

Where is he now?
There were fifteen years between us two
That night I strained to hear the bells
Of a sleigh of the mind and heard him pedal

Into our lane, get off at the gable,
Steady his Raleigh bicycle
Against the whitewash, stand to make sure
The house was quiet, knock at the door

And hand his parcel to a peering woman:
'I suppose you thought I was never coming.'
Eric, tonight I saw it all
Like shadows on your workshop wall,

Smelled wood shavings under the bench,
Weighed the cold steel monkey-wrench
In my soft hand, then stood at the road
To watch your wavering tail-light fade

And knew that if we met again
In an Ulster twilight we would begin
And end whatever we might say
In a speech all toys and carpentry,

A doorstep courtesy to shun
Your father's uniform and gun,
But – now that I have said it out –
Maybe none the worse for that.

A Bat on the Road

A batlike soul waking to consciousness of itself in
darkness and secrecy and loneliness.

You would hoist an old hat on the tines of a fork
and trawl the mouth of the bridge for the slight
bat-thump and flutter. Skinny downy webs,

babynails clawing the sweatband... But don't
bring it down, don't break its flight again,
don't deny it; this time let it go free.

Follow its bat-flap under the stone bridge,
under the Midland and Scottish Railway
and lose it there in the dark.

Next thing it shadows moonslicked laurels
or skims the lapped net on a tennis court.
Next thing it's ahead of you in the road.

What are you after? You keep swerving off,
flying blind over ashpits and netting wire;
invited by the brush of a word like *peignoir*,

rustles and glimpses, shot silk, the stealth of floods
So close to me I could hear her breathing
and there by the lighted window behind trees

it hangs in creepers matting the brickwork
and now it's a wet leaf blowing in the drive,
now soft-deckled, shadow-convolvulus

by the White Gates. Who would have thought it? At
   the White Gates
She let them do whatever they liked. Cling there
as long as you want. There is nothing to hide.

A Hazel Stick for Catherine Ann

The living mother-of-pearl of a salmon
just out of the water

is gone just like that, but your stick
is kept salmon-silver.

Seasoned and bendy,
it convinces the hand

that what you have you hold
to play with and pose with

and lay about with.
But then too it points back to cattle

and spatter and beating
the bars of a gate –

the very stick we might cut
from your family tree.

The living cobalt of an afternoon
dragonfly drew my eye to it first

and the evening I trimmed it for you
you saw your first glow-worm –

all of us stood round in silence, even you
gigantic enough to darken the sky

for a glow-worm.
And when I poked open the grass

a tiny brightening den lit the eye
in the blunt cut end of your stick.

A Kite for Michael and Christopher

All through that Sunday afternoon
a kite flew above Sunday,
a tightened drumhead, an armful of blown chaff.

I'd seen it grey and slippy in the making,
I'd tapped it when it dried out white and stiff,
I'd tied the bows of newspaper
along its six-foot tail.

But now it was far up like a small black lark
and now it dragged as if the bellied string
were a wet rope hauled upon
to lift a shoal.

My friend says that the human soul
is about the weight of a snipe
yet the soul at anchor there,
the string that sags and ascends,
weigh like a furrow assumed into the heavens.

Before the kite plunges down into the wood
and this line goes useless
take in your two hands, boys, and feel
the strumming, rooted, long-tailed pull of grief.
You were born fit for it.
Stand in here in front of me
and take the strain.

The Railway Children

When we climbed the slopes of the cutting
We were eye-level with the white cups
Of the telegraph poles and the sizzling wires.

Like lovely freehand they curved for miles
East and miles west beyond us, sagging
Under their burden of swallows.

We were small and thought we knew nothing
Worth knowing. We thought words travelled the wires
In the shiny pouches of raindrops,

Each one seeded full with the light
Of the sky, the gleam of the lines, and ourselves
So infinitesimally scaled

We could stream through the eye of a needle.

Sweetpea

'What did Thought do?'
                    'Stuck
a feather in the ground and thought
it would grow a hen.'
                    Rod
by rod we pegged the drill for sweetpea
with light brittle sticks,
twiggy and unlikely in fresh mould,
and stalk by stalk we snipped
the coming blooms.

                    And so when pain
had haircracked her old constant vestal stare
I reached for straws and thought:
seeing the sky through a mat of creepers,
like water in the webs of a green net,
opened a clearing where her heart sang
without caution or embarrassment, once or twice.

An Aisling in the Burren

A time was to come when we yearned
for the eel-drugged flats and dunes
of a northern shore, its dulse and its seabirds,
its divisions of brine-maddened grass
pouring over dykes to secure
the aftermath of the reign of the meek.
That was as much of hope that the purest
and saddest were prepared to allow for.

Out of those scenes she arrived, not from a shell
but licked with the wet cold fires of St Elmo,
angel of the last chance, teaching us
the fish in the rock, the fern's
bewildered tenderness deep in the fissure.

That day the clatter of stones
as we climbed was a sermon
on conscience and healing,
her tears a startling deer
on the site of catastrophe.

Widgeon

for Paul Muldoon

It had been badly shot.
While he was plucking it
he found, he says, the voice box –

like a flute stop
in the broken windpipe –

and blew upon it
unexpectedly
his own small widgeon cries.

Sheelagh na Gig

at Kilpeck

I

We look up at her
hunkered into her angle
under the eaves.

She bears the whole stone burden
on the small of her back and shoulders
and pinioned elbows,

the astute mouth, the gripping fingers
saying push, push hard,
push harder.

As the hips go high
her big tadpole forehead
is rounded out in sunlight.

And here beside her are two birds,
a rabbit's head, a ram's,
a mouth devouring heads.

II

Her hands holding herself
are like hands in an old barn
holding a bag open.

I was outside looking in
at its lapped and supple mouth
running grain.

I looked up under the thatch

at the dark mouth and eye
of a bird's nest or a rat hole,

smelling the rose on the wall,
mildew, an earthen floor,
the warm depth of the eaves.

And then one night in the yard
I stood still under heavy rain
wearing the bag like a caul.

III

We look up to her,
her ring-fort eyes,
her little slippy shoulders,

her nose incised and flat,
and feel light-headed looking up.
She is twig-boned, saddle-sexed,

grown-up, grown ordinary,
seeming to say,
'Yes, look at me to your heart's content

but look at every other thing.'
And here is a leaper in a kilt,
two figures kissing,

a mouth with sprigs,
a running hart, two fishes,
a damaged beast with an instrument.

The Loaning

I

As I went down the loaning
the wind shifting in the hedge was like
an old one's whistling speech. And I knew
I was in the limbo of lost words.

They had flown there from raftered sheds and crossroads,
from the shelter of gable ends and turned-up carts.
I saw them streaming out of birch-white throats
and fluttering above iron bedsteads
until the soul would leave the body.
Then on a day close as a stranger's breath
they rose in smoky clouds on the summer sky
and settled in the uvulae of stones
and the soft lungs of the hawthorn.

Then I knew why from the beginning
the loaning breathed on me, breathed even now
in a shiver of beaded gossamers
and the spit blood of a last few haws and rose-hips.

II

Big voices in the womanless kitchen.
They never lit a lamp in the summertime
but took the twilight as it came
like solemn trees. They sat on in the dark
with their pipes red in their mouths, the talk come down
to *Aye* and *Aye* again and, when the dog shifted,
a curt *There boy!* I closed my eyes
to make the light motes stream behind them
and my head went airy, my chair rode
high and low among branches and the wind
stirred up a rookery in the next long *Aye*.

III

Stand still. You can hear
everything going on. High-tension cables
singing above cattle, tractors, barking dogs,
juggernauts changing gear a mile away.
And always the surface noise of the earth
you didn't know you'd heard till a twig snapped
and a blackbird's startled volubility
stopped short.

             When you are tired or terrified
your voice slips back into its old first place
and makes the sound your shades make there...
When Dante snapped a twig in the bleeding wood
a voice sighed out of blood that bubbled up
like sap at the end of green sticks on a fire.

At the click of a cell lock somewhere now
the interrogator steels his *introibo*,
the light motes blaze, a blood-red cigarette
startles the shades, screeching and beseeching.

The Sandpit

1. *1946*

The first hole neat as a trapdoor
cut into grazing and
cut again as the heft and lift
begin, the plate scrabs field-stones
and a tremor blunts in the shaft
at small come-uppances meeting
the driven edge.
        Worms and starlight,
mould-balm on the passing cyclist's face.
The rat's nose in the plastered verge
where they walked to clean their boots.

2. *The Demobbed Bricklayer*

A fence post trimmed and packed
into place, but out of place:
        the soldier
not a soldier any more and never
quite a soldier, what has he
walked into? This is not the desert
night among cold ambulances,
not the absolute sand
of the world, the sun's whip
and grid –
        this sand,
this lustre in their heavy land
is greedy coppers hammered
in the wishing tree of their talk,
the damp ore of money.
        Freckled

and demobbed, worked on like the soil
he is inhaling, he stands
remembering his trade, the song
of his trowel dressing a brickbat,
the tock and tap of its butt, the plumb-
line's certitude, the merriment
in the spirit level's eye.

3. *The Sand Boom*

A fortune in sand then. Sandpits and sandbeds.
River gravel drying in the brickyards.
Clay-scabbed flints, skimming stones of slate,
sandstone pebbles, birds' eggs of flecked granite
all rattled in the caked iron mouth
of the concrete mixer.
                              The first spadeful I saw
pitched up, the handful of gravel
I flung over the cribs,
until they burn in the fireball
or crumble at the edge of the blast
or drink the rain again on their flattened site,
are bonded and set to register
whatever beams and throbs into the wall.
Like undead grains in a stranded cockle shell.
Boulders listening behind the waterfall.

And this as well:
                      foxgloves and saplings
on the worked-out pit floor, grass on the cracked
earth face, anglers nested in an overgrown
loading bay above the deepened stream.

4. *What the Brick Keeps*

His touch, his daydream of the tanks,
his point of vantage on the scaffolding
over chimneys and close hills at noontime,
the constant sound of hidden river water
the new estate rose up through –
with one chop of the trowel he sent it all
into the brick for ever.
It has not stopped travelling in
in the van of all that followed:
floors hammered down, the pipes' first
gulping flow, phone wires and flags
alive on the gable, a bedhead
thumping quickly, banged doors shaking
the joists, rippling the very roof tank.
And my own hands, the size of a grandchild's,
go in there, cold and wet, and my big gaze
at the sandpit opening by the minute.

The King of the Ditchbacks

for John Montague

I

As if a trespasser
unbolted a forgotten gate
and ripped the growth
tangling its lower bars –

just beyond the hedge
he has opened a dark morse
along the bank,
a crooked wounding

of silent, cobwebbed
grass. If I stop
he stops
like the moon.

He lives in his feet
and ears, weather-eyed,
all pad and listening,
a denless mover.

Under the bridge
his reflection shifts
sideways to the current,
mothy, alluring.

I am haunted
by his stealthy rustling,
the unexpected spoor,
the pollen settling.

II

I was sure I knew him. The time I'd spent obsessively
in that upstairs room bringing myself close to him:
each entranced hiatus as I chainsmoked and stared
out the dormer into the grassy hillside I was laying
myself open. He was depending on me as I hung out
on the limb of a translated phrase like a youngster
dared out on to an alder branch over the whirlpool.
Small dreamself in the branches. Dream fears I
inclined towards, interrogating:

— Are you the one I ran upstairs to find drowned
  under running water in the bath?
— The one the mowing machine severed like a
  hare in the stiff frieze of harvest?
— Whose little bloody clothes we buried in
  the garden?
— The one who lay awake in darkness a wall's
  breadth from the troubled hoofs?

After I had dared these invocations, I went back
towards the gate to follow him. And my stealth was
second nature to me, as if I were coming into my
own. I remembered I had been vested for this calling.

III

When I was taken aside that day
I had the sense of election:

they dressed my head in a fishnet
and plaited leafy twigs through meshes

so my vision was a bird's
at the heart of a thicket

and I spoke as I moved
like a voice from a shaking bush.

King of the ditchbacks,
I went with them obediently

to the edge of a pigeon wood –
deciduous canopy, screened wain of evening

we lay beneath in silence.
No birds came, but I waited

among briars and stones, or whispered
or broke the watery gossamers

if I moved a muscle.
'Come back to us,' they said, 'in harvest,

when we hide in the stooked corn,
when the gundogs can hardly retrieve

what's brought down.' And I saw myself
rising to move in that dissimulation,

top-knotted, masked in sheaves, noting
the fall of birds: a rich young man

leaving everything he had
for a migrant solitude.

PART TWO:
STATION ISLAND

PART TWO
SILICON ISLAND

Station Island

I

A hurry of bell-notes
flew over morning hush
and water-blistered cornfields,
an escaped ringing
that stopped as quickly

as it started. *Sunday,*
the silence breathed
and could not settle back
for a man had appeared
at the side of the field

with a bow-saw, held
stiffly up like a lyre.
He moved and stopped to gaze
up into hazel bushes,
angled his saw in,

pulled back to gaze again
and move on to the next.
'I know you, Simon Sweeney,
for an old Sabbath-breaker
who has been dead for years.'

'Damn all you know,' he said,
his eye still on the hedge
and not turning his head.
'I was your mystery man
and am again this morning.

Through gaps in the bushes,
your First Communion face
would watch me cutting timber.

When cut or broken limbs
of trees went yellow, when

woodsmoke sharpened air
or ditches rustled
you sensed my trail there
as if it had been sprayed.
It left you half afraid.

When they bade you listen
in the bedroom dark
to wind and rain in the trees
and think of tinkers camped
under a heeled-up cart

you shut your eyes and saw
a wet axle and spokes
in moonlight, and me
streaming from the shower,
headed for your door.'

Sunlight broke in the hazels,
the quick bell-notes began
a second time. I turned
at another sound:
a crowd of shawled women

were wading the young corn,
their skirts brushing softly.
Their motion saddened morning.
It whispered to the silence,
'Pray for us, pray for us,'

it conjured through the air
until the field was full
of half-remembered faces,
a loosed congregation
that straggled past and on.

As I drew behind them
I was a fasted pilgrim,
light-headed, leaving home
to face into my station.
'Stay clear of all processions!'

Sweeney shouted at me
but the murmur of the crowd
and their feet slushing through
the tender, bladed growth
opened a drugged path

I was set upon.
I trailed those early-risers
who had fallen into step
before the smokes were up.
The quick bell rang again.

II

I was parked on a high road, listening
to peewits and wind blowing round the car
when something came to life in the driving mirror,

someone walking fast in an overcoat
and boots, bareheaded, big, determined
in his sure haste along the crown of the road

so that I felt myself the challenged one.
The car door slammed. I was suddenly out
face to face with an aggravated man

raving on about nights spent listening for
gun butts to come cracking on the door,
yeomen on the rampage, and his neighbour

among them, hammering home the shape of things.
'Round about here you overtook the women,'
I said, as the thing came clear. 'Your *Lough Derg Pilgrim*

haunts me every time I cross this mountain –
as if I am being followed, or following.
I'm on my road there now to do the station.'

'O holy Jesus Christ, does nothing change?'
His head jerked sharply side to side and up
like a diver surfacing,

then with a look that said, *who is this cub
anyhow*, he took cognizance again
of where he was: the road, the mountain top,

and the air, softened by a shower of rain,
worked on his anger visibly until:
'It is a road you travel on your own.

I who learned to read in the reek of flax
and smelled hanged bodies rotting on their gibbets
and saw their looped slime gleaming from the sacks –

hard-mouthed Ribbonmen and Orange bigots
made me into the old fork-tongued turncoat
who mucked the byre of their politics.

If times were hard, I could be hard too.
I made the traitor in me sink the knife.
And maybe there's a lesson there for you,

whoever you are, wherever you come out of,
for though there's something natural in your smile
there's something in it strikes me as defensive.'

'I have no mettle for the angry role,'
I said. 'I come from County Derry,
born in earshot of an Hibernian hall

where a band of Ribbonmen played hymns to Mary.
By then the brotherhood was a frail procession
staggering home drunk on Patrick's Day

in collarettes and sashes fringed with green.
Obedient strains like theirs tuned me first
and not that harp of unforgiving iron

the Fenians strung. A lot of what you wrote
I heard and did: this Lough Derg station,
flax-pullings, dances, summer crossroads chat

and the shaky local voice of education.
All that. And always, Orange drums.
And neighbours on the roads at night with guns.'

'I know, I know, I know, I know,' he said,

'but you have to try to make sense of what comes.
Remember everything and keep your head.'

'The alders in the hedge,' I said, 'mushrooms,
dark-clumped grass where cows or horses dunged,
the cluck when pith-lined chestnut shells split open

in your hand, the melt of shells corrupting,
old jampots in a drain clogged up with mud –'
But now Carleton was interrupting:

'All this is like a trout kept in a spring
or maggots sown in wounds –
another life that cleans our element.

We are earthworms of the earth, and all that
has gone through us is what will be our trace.'
He turned on his heel when he was saying this

and headed up the road at the same hard pace.

III

I knelt. Hiatus. Habit's afterlife...
I was back among bead clicks and the murmurs
from inside confessionals, side altars
where candles died insinuating slight

intimate smells of wax at body heat.
There was an active, wind-stilled hush, as if
in a shell the listened-for ocean stopped
and a tide rested and sustained the roof.

A seaside trinket floated then and idled
in vision, like phosphorescent weed,
a toy grotto with seedling mussel shells
and cockles glued in patterns over it,

pearls condensed from a child invalid's breath
into a shimmering ark, my house of gold
that housed the snowdrop weather of her death
long ago. I would stow away in the hold

of our big oak sideboard and forage for it
laid past in its tissue paper for good.
It was like touching birds' eggs, robbing the nest
of the word *wreath*, as kept and dry and secret

as her name which they hardly ever spoke
but was a white bird trapped inside me
beating scared wings when *Health of the Sick*
fluttered its *pray for us* in the litany.

A cold draught blew under the kneeling boards.
I thought of walking round
and round a space utterly empty,
utterly a source, like the idea of sound;

like an absence stationed in the swamp-fed air
above a ring of walked-down grass and rushes
where we once found the bad carcass and scrags of hair
of our dog that had disappeared weeks before.

IV

Blurred swimmings as I faced the sun, my back
to the stone pillar and the iron cross,
ready to say the dream words *I renounce*...

Blurred oval prints of newly ordained faces,
'Father' pronounced with a fawning relish,
the sunlit tears of parents being blessed.

I met a young priest, glossy as a blackbird,
as if he had stepped from his anointing
a moment ago: his purple stole and cord

or cincture tied loosely, his polished shoes
unexpectedly secular beneath
a pleated, lace-hemmed alb of linen cloth.

His name had lain undisturbed for years
like an old bicycle wheel in a ditch
ripped at last from under jungling briars,

wet and perished. My arms were open wide
but I could not say the words. 'The rain forest,' he said,
'you've never seen the like of it. I lasted

only a couple of years. Bare-breasted
women and rat-ribbed men. Everything wasted.
I rotted like a pear. I sweated masses...'

His breath came short and shorter. 'In long houses
I raised the chalice above headdresses.
In hoc signo... On that abandoned

mission compound, my vocation
is a steam off drenched creepers.'
I had broken off from the renunciation

while he was speaking, to clear the way
for other pilgrims queueing to get started.
'I'm older now than you when you went away,'

I ventured, feeling a strange reversal.
'I never could see you on the foreign missions.
I could only see you on a bicycle,

a clerical student home for the summer
doomed to the decent thing. Visiting neighbours.
Drinking tea and praising home-made bread.

Something in them would be ratified
when they saw you at the door in your black suit,
arriving like some sort of holy mascot.

You gave too much relief, you raised a siege
the world had laid against their kitchen grottoes
hung with holy pictures and crucifixes.'

'And you,' he faltered, 'what are you doing here
but the same thing? What possessed you?
I at least was young and unaware

that what I thought was chosen was convention.
But all this you were clear of you walked into
over again. And the god has, as they say, withdrawn.

What are you doing, going through these motions?
Unless... Unless...' Again he was short of breath
and his whole fevered body yellowed and shook.

'Unless you are here taking the last look.'
Suddenly where he stood was bare as the roads
we both had grown up beside, where a sick man

had taken his last look one drizzly evening
when steam rose like the first breath of spring,
a knee-deep mist I waded silently

behind him, on his circuits, visiting.

V

An old man's hands, like soft paws rowing forward,
groped for and warded off the air ahead.
Barney Murphy shuffled on the concrete.
Master Murphy. I heard the weakened voice
bulling in sudden rage all over again
and fell in behind, my eyes fixed on his heels
like a man lifting swathes at a mower's heels.
His sockless feet were like the dried broad bean
that split its stitches in the display jar
high on a window in the old classroom,
white as shy faces in the classroom door.
'Master,' those elders whispered, 'I wonder, master...'
rustling envelopes, proffering them, withdrawing,
and 'Master' I repeated to myself
so that he stopped but did not turn or move,
his shoulders gone quiet and small, his head
vigilant in the cold gusts off the lough.
I moved ahead and faced him, shook his hand.

Above the winged collar, his mottled face
went distant in a smile as the voice
readied itself and husked and scraped, 'Good man,
good man yourself,' before it lapsed again
in the limbo and dry urn of the larynx.
The adam's apple in its weathered sac
worked like the plunger of a pump in drought
but yielded nothing to help the helpless smile.
Morning field smells came past on the wind,
the sex-cut of sweetbriar after rain,
new-mown meadow hay, bird's nests filled with leaves.
'You'd have thought that Anahorish School
was purgatory enough for any man,'
I said. 'You've done your station.'
Then a little trembling happened and his breath
rushed the air softly as scythes in his lost meadows.

'Birch trees have overgrown Leitrim Moss,
dairy herds are grazing where the school was
and the school garden's loose black mould is grass.'
He was gone with that and I was faced wrong way
into more pilgrims absorbed in this exercise.
As I stood among their whispers and bare feet
the mists of all the mornings I set out
for Latin classes with him, face to face,
refreshed me. *Mensa, mensa, mensam*
sang in the air like a busy whetstone.

'We'll go some day to my uncle's farm at Toome –'
Another master spoke. '*For what is the great
moving power and spring of verse? Feeling, and
in particular, love.*When I went last year
I drank three cups of water from the well.
It was very cold. It stung me in the ears.
You should have met him –' Coming in as usual
with the rubbed quotation and his cocked bird's eye
dabbing for detail. *When you're on the road
give lifts to people, you'll always learn something.*
There he went, in his belted gaberdine,
and after him, a third fosterer,
slack-shouldered and clear-eyed: 'Sure I might have known
once I had made the pad, you'd be after me
sooner or later. Forty-two years on
and you've got no farther! But after that again,
where else would you go? Iceland, maybe? Maybe the
    Dordogne?'
And then the parting shot. 'In my own day
the odd one came here on the hunt for women.'

VI

Freckle-face, fox-head, pod of the broom,
Catkin-pixie, little fern-swish:
Where did she arrive from?
Like a wish wished
And gone, her I chose at 'secrets'
And whispered to. When we were playing houses.
I was sunstruck at the basilica door –
A stillness far away, a space, a dish,
A blackened tin and knocked over stool –
Like a tramped neolithic floor
Uncovered among dunes where the bent grass
Whispers on like reeds about Midas's
*Secrets, secrets.*I shut my ears to the bell.
Head hugged. Eyes shut. Leaf ears. *Don't tell. Don't tell.*

A stream of pilgrims answering the bell
Trailed up the steps as I went down them
Towards the bottle-green, still
Shade of an oak. Shades of the Sabine farm
On the beds of Saint Patrick's Purgatory.
Late summer, country distance, not an air:
Loosen the toga for wine and poetry
Till Phoebus returning routs the morning star.
As a somnolent hymn to Mary rose
I felt an old pang that bags of grain
And the sloped shafts of forks and hoes
Once mocked me with, at my own long virgin
Fasts and thirsts, my nightly shadow feasts,
Haunting the granaries of words like *breasts.*

As if I knelt for years at a keyhole
Mad for it, and all that ever opened
Was the breathed-on grille of a confessional
Until that night I saw her honey-skinned
Shoulder-blades and the wheatlands of her back

Through the wide keyhole of her keyhole dress
And a window facing the deep south of luck
Opened and I inhaled the land of kindness.
As little flowers that were all bowed and shut
By the night chills rise on their stems and open
As soon as they have felt the touch of sunlight,
So I revived in my own wilting powers
And my heart flushed, like somebody set free.
Translated, given, under the oak tree.

VII

I had come to the edge of the water,
soothed by just looking, idling over it
as if it were a clear barometer

or a mirror, when his reflection
did not appear but I sensed a presence
entering into my concentration

on not being concentrated as he spoke
my name. And though I was reluctant
I turned to meet his face and the shock

is still in me at what I saw. His brow
was blown open above the eye and blood
had dried on his neck and cheek. 'Easy now,'

he said, 'it's only me. You've seen men as raw
after a football match... What time it was
when I was wakened up I still don't know

but I heard this knocking, knocking, and it
scared me, like the phone in the small hours,
so I had the sense not to put on the light

but looked out from behind the curtain.
I saw two customers on the doorstep
and an old landrover with the doors open

parked on the street so I let the curtain drop;
but they must have been waiting for it to move
for they shouted to come down into the shop.

She started to cry then and roll round the bed,
lamenting and lamenting to herself,
not even asking who it was. "Is your head

astray, or what's come over you?" I roared, more
to bring myself to my senses
than out of any real anger at her

for the knocking shook me, the way they kept it up,
and her whingeing and half-screeching made it worse.
All the time they were shouting, "Shop!

Shop!" so I pulled on my shoes and a sportscoat
and went back to the window and called out,
"What do you want? Could you quieten the racket

or I'll not come down at all." "There's a child not well.
Open up and see what you have got – pills
or a powder or something in a bottle,"

one of them said. He stepped back off the footpath
so I could see his face in the street lamp
and when the other moved I knew them both.

But bad and all as the knocking was, the quiet
hit me worse. She was quiet herself now,
lying dead still, whispering to watch out.

At the bedroom door I switched on the light.
"It's odd they didn't look for a chemist.
Who are they anyway at this time of the night?"

she asked me, with the eyes standing in her head.
"I know them to see," I said, but something
made me reach and squeeze her hand across the bed

before I went downstairs into the aisle
of the shop. I stood there, going weak
in the legs. I remember the stale smell

of cooked meat or something coming through

as I went to open up. From then on
you know as much about it as I do.'

'Did they say nothing?' 'Nothing. What would they say?'
'Were they in uniform? Not masked in any way?'
'They were barefaced as they would be in the day,

shites thinking they were the be-all and the end-all.'
'Not that it is any consolation,
but they were caught,' I told him, 'and got jail.'

Big-limbed, decent, open-faced, he stood
forgetful of everything now except
whatever was welling up in his spoiled head,

beginning to smile. 'You've put on weight
since you did your courting in that big Austin
you got the loan of on a Sunday night.'

Through life and death he had hardly aged.
There always was an athlete's cleanliness
shining off him and except for the ravaged

forehead and the blood, he was still that same
rangy midfielder in a blue jersey
and starched pants, the one stylist on the team,

the perfect, clean, unthinkable victim.
'Forgive the way I have lived indifferent –
forgive my timid circumspect involvement,'

I surprised myself by saying. 'Forgive
my eye,' he said, 'all that's above my head.'
And then a stun of pain seemed to go through him

and he trembled like a heatwave and faded.

VIII

Black water. White waves. Furrows snowcapped.
A magpie flew from the basilica
and staggered in the granite airy space
I was staring into, on my knees
at the hard mouth of St Brigid's Bed.
I came to and there at the bed's stone hub
was my archaeologist, very like himself,
with his scribe's face smiling its straight-lipped smile,
starting at the sight of me with the same old
pretence of amazement, so that the wing
of woodkerne's hair fanned down over his brow.
And then as if a shower were blackening
already blackened stubble, the dark weather
of his unspoken pain came over him.
A pilgrim bent and whispering on his rounds
inside the bed passed between us slowly.

'Those dreamy stars that pulsed across the screen
beside you in the ward – your heartbeats, Tom, I mean –
scared me the way they stripped things naked.
My banter failed too early in that visit.
I could not take my eyes off the machine.
I had to head back straight away to Dublin,
guilty and empty, feeling I had said nothing
and that, as usual, I had somehow broken
covenants, and failed an obligation.
I half-knew we would never meet again...
Did our long gaze and last handshake contain
nothing to appease that recognition?'
'Nothing at all. But familiar stone
had me half-numbed to face the thing alone.
I loved my still-faced archaeology.
The small crab-apple physiognomies
on high crosses, carved heads in abbeys...
Why else dig in for years in that hard place

in a muck of bigotry under the walls
picking through shards and Williamite cannon balls?
But all that we just turned to banter too.
I felt that I should have seen far more of you
and maybe would have – but dead at thirty-two!
Ah poet, lucky poet, tell me why
what seemed deserved and promised passed me by?'

I could not speak. I saw a hoard of black
basalt axe heads, smooth as a beetle's back,
a cairn of stone force that might detonate,
the eggs of danger. And then I saw a face
he had once given me, a plaster cast
of an abbess, done by the Gowran master,
mild-mouthed and cowled, a character of grace.
'Your gift will be a candle in our house.'
But he had gone when I looked to meet his eyes
and hunkering instead there in his place
was a bleeding, pale-faced boy, plastered in mud.
'The red-hot pokers blazed a lovely red
in Jerpoint the Sunday I was murdered,'
he said quietly. 'Now do you remember?
You were there with poets when you got the word
and stayed there with them, while your own flesh and blood
was carted to Bellaghy from the Fews.
They showed more agitation at the news
than you did.'
                            'But they were getting crisis
first-hand, Colum, they had happened in on
live sectarian assassination.
I was dumb, encountering what was destined.'
And so I pleaded with my second cousin.
'I kept seeing a grey stretch of Lough Beg
and the strand empty at daybreak.
I felt like the bottom of a dried-up lake.'

'You saw that, and you wrote that – not the fact.
You confused evasion and artistic tact.

The Protestant who shot me through the head
I accuse directly, but indirectly, you
who now atone perhaps upon this bed
for the way you whitewashed ugliness and drew
the lovely blinds of the *Purgatorio*
and saccharined my death with morning dew.'

Then I seemed to waken out of sleep
among more pilgrims whom I did not know
drifting to the hostel for the night.

IX

'My brain dried like spread turf, my stomach
Shrank to a cinder and tightened and cracked.
Often I was dogs on my own track
Of blood on wet grass that I could have licked.
Under the prison blanket, an ambush
Stillness I felt safe in settled round me.
Street lights came on in small towns, the bomb flash
Came before the sound, I saw country
I knew from Glenshane down to Toome
And heard a car I could make out years away
With me in the back of it like a white-faced groom,
A hit-man on the brink, emptied and deadly.
When the police yielded my coffin, I was light
As my head when I took aim.'

                             This voice from blight
And hunger died through the black dorm:
There he was, laid out with a drift of mass cards
At his shrouded feet. Then the firing party's
Volley in the yard. I saw woodworm
In gate posts and door jambs, smelt mildew
From the byre loft where he watched and hid
From fields his draped coffin would raft through.
Unquiet soul, they should have buried you
In the bog where you threw your first grenade,
Where only helicopters and curlews
Make their maimed music, and sphagnum moss
Could teach you its medicinal repose
Until, when the weasel whistles on its tail,
No other weasel will obey its call.

I dreamt and drifted. All seemed to run to waste
As down a swirl of mucky, glittering flood
Strange polyp floated like a huge corrupt
Magnolia bloom, surreal as a shed breast,
My softly awash and blanching self-disgust.

And I cried among night waters, 'I repent
My unweaned life that kept me competent
To sleepwalk with connivance and mistrust.'
Then, like a pistil growing from the polyp,
A lighted candle rose and steadied up
Until the whole bright-masted thing retrieved
A course and the currents it had gone with
Were what it rode and showed. No more adrift,
My feet touched bottom and my heart revived.

Then something round and clear
And mildly turbulent, like a bubbleskin
Or a moon in smoothly rippled lough water
Rose in a cobwebbed space: the molten
Inside-sheen of an instrument
Revolved its polished convexes full
Upon me, so close and brilliant
I pitched backwards in a headlong fall.
And then it was the clarity of waking
To sunlight and a bell and gushing taps
In the next cubicle. Still there for the taking!
The old brass trumpet with its valves and stops
I found once in loft thatch, a mystery
I shied from then for I thought such trove beyond me.

'I hate how quick I was to know my place.
I hate where I was born, hate everything
That made me biddable and unforthcoming,'
I mouthed at my half-composed face
In the shaving mirror, like somebody
Drunk in the bathroom during a party,
Lulled and repelled by his own reflection.
As if the cairnstone could defy the cairn.
As if the eddy could reform the pool.
As if a stone swirled under a cascade,
Eroded and eroding in its bed,
Could grind itself down to a different core.
Then I thought of the tribe whose dances never fail
For they keep dancing till they sight the deer.

X

Morning stir in the hostel. A pot
hooked on forged links. Soot flakes. Plumping water.
The open door letting in sunlight.
Hearthsmoke rambling and a thud of earthenware

drumming me back until I saw the mug
beyond my reach on its high shelf, the one
patterned with cornflowers, blue sprig after sprig
repeating round it, as quiet as a milestone,

old and glazed and haircracked. It had stood for years
in its patient sheen and turbulent atoms,
unchallenging, unremembered *lars*
I seemed to waken to and waken from.

When had it not been there? There was one night
when the fit-up actors used it for a prop
and I sat in a dark hall estranged from it
as a couple vowed and called it their loving cup

and held it in our gaze until the curtain
jerked shut with an ordinary noise.
Dipped and glamoured from this translation,
it was restored with all its cornflower haze

still dozing, its parchment glazes fast –
as the otter surfaced once with Ronan's psalter
miraculously unharmed, that had been lost
a day and a night under lough water.

And so the saint praised God on the lough shore.
The dazzle of the impossible suddenly
blazed across the threshold, a sun-glare
to put out the small hearths of constancy.

XI

As if the prisms of the kaleidoscope
I plunged once in a butt of muddied water
surfaced like a marvellous lightship

and out of its silted crystals a monk's face
that had spoken years ago from behind a grille
spoke again about the need and chance

to salvage everything, to re-envisage
the zenith and glimpsed jewels of any gift
mistakenly abased...

What came to nothing could always be replenished.
'Read poems as prayers,' he said, 'and for your penance
translate me something by Juan de la Cruz.'

Returned from Spain to our chapped wilderness,
his consonants aspirate, his forehead shining,
he had made me feel there was nothing to confess.

Now his sandalled passage stirred me on to this:
How well I know that fountain, filling, running,
        although it is the night.

That eternal fountain, hidden away,
I know its haven and its secrecy
        although it is the night.

But not its source because it does not have one,
which is all sources' source and origin
        although it is the night.

No other thing can be so beautiful.
Here the earth and heaven drink their fill
        although it is the night.

So pellucid it never can be muddied,
and I know that all light radiates from it
    although it is the night.

I know no sounding-line can find its bottom,
nobody ford or plumb its deepest fathom
    although it is the night.

And its current so in flood it overspills
to water hell and heaven and all peoples
    although it is the night.

And the current that is generated there,
as far as it wills to, it can flow that far
    although it is the night.

And from these two a third current proceeds
which neither of these two, I know, precedes
    although it is the night.

This eternal fountain hides and splashes
within this living bread that is life to us
    although it is the night.

Hear it calling out to every creature.
And they drink these waters, although it is dark here
    because it is the night.

I am repining for this living fountain.
Within this bread of life I see it plain
    although it is the night.

XII

Like a convalescent, I took the hand
stretched down from the jetty, sensed again
an alien comfort as I stepped on ground

to find the helping hand still gripping mine,
fish-cold and bony, but whether to guide
or to be guided I could not be certain

for the tall man in step at my side
seemed blind, though he walked straight as a rush
upon his ash plant, his eyes fixed straight ahead.

Then I knew him in the flesh
out there on the tarmac among the cars,
wintered hard and sharp as a blackthorn bush.

His voice eddying with the vowels of all rivers
came back to me, though he did not speak yet,
a voice like a prosecutor's or a singer's,

cunning, narcotic, mimic, definite
as a steel nib's downstroke, quick and clean,
and suddenly he hit a litter basket

with his stick, saying, 'Your obligation
is not discharged by any common rite.
What you must do must be done on your own

so get back in harness. The main thing is to write
for the joy of it. Cultivate a work-lust
that imagines its haven like your hands at night

dreaming the sun in the sunspot of a breast.
You are fasted now, light-headed, dangerous.
Take off from here. And don't be so earnest,

let others wear the sackcloth and the ashes.
Let go, let fly, forget.
You've listened long enough. Now strike your note.'

It was as if I had stepped free into space
alone with nothing that I had not known
already. Raindrops blew in my face

as I came to. 'Old father, mother's son,
there is a moment in Stephen's diary
for April the thirteenth, a revelation

set among my stars – that one entry
has been a sort of password in my ears,
the collect of a new epiphany,

the Feast of the Holy Tundish.' 'Who cares,'
he jeered, 'any more? The English language
belongs to us. You are raking at dead fires,

a waste of time for somebody your age.
That subject people stuff is a cod's game,
infantile, like your peasant pilgrimage.

You lose more of yourself than you redeem
doing the decent thing. Keep at a tangent.
When they make the circle wide, it's time to swim

out on your own and fill the element
with signatures on your own frequency,
echo soundings, searches, probes, allurements,

elver-gleams in the dark of the whole sea.'
The shower broke in a cloudburst, the tarmac
fumed and sizzled. As he moved off quickly

the downpour loosed its screens round his straight walk.

PART THREE:
SWEENEY REDIVIVUS

The First Gloss

Take hold of the shaft of the pen.
Subscribe to the first step taken
from a justified line
into the margin.

Sweeney Redivivus

I stirred wet sand and gathered myself
to climb the steep-flanked mound,
my head like a ball of wet twine
dense with soakage, but beginning
to unwind.
                    Another smell
was blowing off the river, bitter
as night airs in a scutch mill.
The old trees were nowhere,
the hedges thin as penwork
and the whole enclosure lost
under hard paths and sharp-ridged houses.

And there I was, incredible to myself,
among people far too eager to believe me
and my story, even if it happened to be true.

Unwinding

If the twine unravels to the very end
the stuff gathering under my fingernails
is being picked off whitewash at the bedside.

And the stuff gathering in my ear
is their sex-pruned and unfurtherable
moss-talk, incubated under lamplight,

which will have to be unlearned
even though from there on everything
is going to be learning.

So the twine unwinds and loosely widens
backward through areas that forwarded
understandings of all I would undertake.

In the Beech

I was a lookout posted and forgotten.

On one side under me, the concrete road.
On the other, the bullocks' covert,
the breath and plaster of a drinking place
where the school-leaver discovered peace
to touch himself in the reek of churned-up mud.

And the tree itself a strangeness and a comfort,
as much a column as a bole. The very ivy
puzzled its milk-tooth frills and tapers
over the grain: was it bark or masonry?

I watched the red-brick chimney rear
its stamen course by course,
and the steeplejacks up there at their antics
like flies against the mountain.

I felt the tanks' advance beginning
at the cynosure of the growth rings,
then winced at their imperium refreshed
in each powdered bolt mark on the concrete.
And the pilot with his goggles back came in
so low I could see the cockpit rivets.

My hidebound boundary tree. My tree of knowledge.
My thick-tapped, soft-fledged, airy listening post.

The First Kingdom

The royal roads were cow paths.
The queen mother hunkered on a stool
and played the harpstrings of milk
into a wooden pail.
With seasoned sticks the nobles
lorded it over the hindquarters of cattle.

Units of measurement were pondered
by the cartful, barrowful and bucketful.
Time was a backward rote of names and mishaps,
bad harvests, fires, unfair settlements,
deaths in floods, murders and miscarriages.

And if my rights to it all came only
by their acclamation, what was it worth?
I blew hot and blew cold.
They were two-faced and accommodating.
And seed, breed and generation still
they are holding on, every bit
as pious and exacting and demeaned.

The First Flight

It was more sleepwalk than spasm
yet that was a time when the times
were also in spasm —

the ties and the knots running through us
split open
down the lines of the grain.

As I drew close to pebbles and berries,
the smell of wild garlic, relearning
the acoustic of frost

and the meaning of woodnote,
my shadow over the field
was only a spin-off,

my empty place an excuse
for shifts in the camp, old rehearsals
of debts and betrayal.

Singly they came to the tree
with a stone in each pocket
to whistle and bill me back in

and I would collide and cascade
through leaves when they left,
my point of repose knocked askew.

I was mired in attachment
until they began to pronounce me
a feeder off battlefields

so I mastered new rungs of the air
to survey out of reach

their bonfires on hills, their hosting

and fasting, the levies from Scotland
as always, and the people of art
diverting their rhythmical chants

to fend off the onslaught of winds
I would welcome and climb
at the top of my bent.

Drifting Off

The guttersnipe and the albatross
gliding for days without a single wingbeat
were equally beyond me.

I yearned for the gannet's strike,
the unbegrudging concentration
of the heron.

In the camaraderie of rookeries,
in the spiteful vigilance of colonies
I was at home.

I learned to distrust
the allure of the cuckoo
and the gossip of starlings,

kept faith with doughty bullfinches,
levelled my wit too often
to the small-minded wren

and too often caved in
to the pathos of waterhens
and panicky corncrakes.

I gave much credence to stragglers,
overrated the composure of blackbirds
and the folklore of magpies.

But when goldfinch or kingfisher rent
the veil of the usual,
pinions whispered and braced

as I stooped, unwieldy
and brimming,
my spurs at the ready.

Alerted

From the start I was lucky
and challenged, always whacked down
to make sure I would not grow up
too hopeful and trusting –

I was asking myself could I ever
and if ever I should
outstrip obedience, when I heard
the bark of the vixen in heat.

She carded the webs of desire,
she disinterred gutlines and lightning,
she broke the ice of demure
and exemplary stars –

and rooted me to the spot,
alerted, disappointed
under my old clandestine
pre-Copernican night.

The Cleric

I heard new words prayed at cows
in the byre, found his sign
on the crock and the hidden still,

smelled fumes from his censer
in the first smokes of morning.
Next thing he was making a progress

through gaps, stepping out sites,
sinking his crozier deep
in the fort-hearth.

If he had stuck to his own
cramp-jawed abbesses and intoners
dibbling round the enclosure,

his Latin and blather of love,
his parchments and scheming
in letters shipped over water –

but no, he overbore
with his unctions and orders,
he had to get in on the ground.

History that planted its standards
on his gables and spires
ousted me to the marches

of skulking and whingeing.
Or did I desert?
Give him his due, in the end

he opened my path to a kingdom
of such scope and neuter allegiance
my emptiness reigns at its whim.

The Hermit

As he prowled the rim of his clearing
where the blade of choice had not spared
one stump of affection

he was like a ploughshare
interred to sustain the whole field
of force, from the bitted

and high-drawn sideways curve
of the horse's neck to the aim
held fast in the wrists and elbows –

the more brutal the pull
and the drive, the deeper
and quieter the work of refreshment.

The Master

He dwelt in himself
like a rook in an unroofed tower.

To get close I had to maintain
a climb up deserted ramparts
and not flinch, not raise an eye
to search for an eye on the watch
from his coign of seclusion.

Deliberately he would unclasp
his book of withholding
a page at a time and it was nothing
arcane, just the old rules
we all had inscribed on our slates.
Each character blocked on the parchment secure
in its volume and measure.
Each maxim given its space.

Like quarrymen's hammers and wedges proofed
by intransigent service.
Like coping stones where you rest
in the balm of the wellspring.

How flimsy I felt climbing down
the unrailed stairs on the wall,
hearing the purpose and venture
in a wingflap above me.

The Scribes

I never warmed to them.
If they were excellent they were petulant
and jaggy as the holly tree
they rendered down for ink.
And if I never belonged among them,
they could never deny me my place.

In the hush of the scriptorium
a black pearl kept gathering in them
like the old dry glut inside their quills.
In the margin of texts of praise
they scratched and clawed.
They snarled if the day was dark
or too much chalk had made the vellum bland
or too little left it oily.

Under the rumps of lettering
they herded myopic angers.
Resentment seeded in the uncurling
fernheads of their capitals.

Now and again I started up
miles away and saw in my absence
the sloped cursive of each back and felt them
perfect themselves against me page by page.

Let them remember this not inconsiderable
contribution to their jealous art.

A Waking Dream

When I made the rush to throw salt
on her tail the long treadles of the air
took me in my stride so I was lofted
beyond exerted breath, the cheep and blur
of trespass and occurrence.
As if one who had dropped off came to
suspecting the very stillness of the sunlight.

In the Chestnut Tree

Body heat under the leaves, matronly
slippage and hoistings

as she spreads in the pool of the day,
a queen in her fifties, dropping

purses and earrings. What does she care
for the lean-shanked and thorny,

old firm-fleshed Susannah, stepped in
over her belly,

parts of her soapy and white,
parts of her blunting?

And the little bird of death
piping and piping somewhere

in her gorgeous tackling? Surely not.
She breathes deep and stirs up the algae.

Sweeney's Returns

The clouds would tatter a moment
over green peninsulas, cattle
far below, the dormant roadways –
and I imagined her clothes half-slipped
off the chair, the dawn-fending blind, her eyelids'
glister and burgeon.

Then when I perched on the sill
to gaze at my coffers of absence
I was like a scout at risk behind lines
who raises his head in a wheatfield
to take a first look, the throb of his breakthrough
going on inside him unstoppably:

the blind was up, a bangle
lay in the sun, the fleshed hyacinth
had begun to divulge.
Where had she gone? Beyond
the tucked and level bed, I floundered
in my wild reflection in the mirror.

Holly

It rained when it should have snowed.
When we went to gather holly

the ditches were swimming, we were wet
to the knees, our hands were all jags

and water ran up our sleeves.
There should have been berries

but the sprigs we brought into the house
gleamed like smashed bottle-glass.

Now here I am, in a room that is decked
with the red-berried, waxy-leafed stuff,

and I almost forget what it's like
to be wet to the skin or longing for snow.

I reach for a book like a doubter
and want it to flare round my hand,

a black-letter bush, a glittering shield-wall
cutting as holly and ice.

An Artist

I love the thought of his anger.
His obstinacy against the rock, his coercion
of the substance from green apples.

The way he was a dog barking
at the image of himself barking.
And his hatred of his own embrace
of working as the only thing that worked –
the vulgarity of expecting ever
gratitude or admiration, which
would mean a stealing from him.

The way his fortitude held and hardened
because he did what he knew.
His forehead like a hurled *boule*
travelling unpainted space
behind the apple and behind the mountain.

The Old Icons

Why, when it was all over, did I hold on to them?

A patriot with folded arms in a shaft of light:
the barred cell window and his sentenced face
are the only bright spots in the little etching.

An oleograph of snowy hills, the outlawed priest's
red vestments, with the redcoats toiling closer
and the lookout coming like a fox across the gaps.

And the old committee of the sedition-mongers,
so well turned out in their clasped brogues and waistcoats,
the legend of their names an informer's list

prepared by neat-cuffs, third from left, at rear,
more compelling than the rest of them,
pivoting an action that was his rack

and others' ruin, the very rhythm of his name
a register of dear-bought treacheries
grown transparent now, and inestimable.

In Illo Tempore

The big missal splayed
and dangled silky ribbons
of emerald and purple and watery white.

Intransitively we would assist,
confess, receive. The verbs
assumed us. We adored.

And we lifted our eyes to the nouns.
Altar stone was dawn and monstrance noon,
the word rubric itself a bloodshot sunset.

Now I live by a famous strand
where seabirds cry in the small hours
like incredible souls

and even the range wall of the promenade
that I press down on for conviction
hardly tempts me to credit it.

On the Road

The road ahead
kept reeling in
at a steady speed,
the verges dripped.

In my hands
like a wrested trophy,
the empty round
of the steering wheel.

The trance of driving
made all roads one:
the seraph-haunted, Tuscan
footpath, the green

oak-alleys of Dordogne
or that track through corn
where the rich young man
asked his question –

*Master, what must I
do to be saved?*
Or the road where the bird
with an earth-red back

and a white and black
tail, like parquet
of flint and jet,
wheeled over me

in visitation.
*Sell all you have
and give to the poor.*
I was up and away

like a human soul
that plumes from the mouth
in undulant, tenor
black-letter Latin.

I was one for sorrow,
Noah's dove,
a panicked shadow
crossing the deerpath.

If I came to earth
it would be by way of
a small east window
I once squeezed through,

scaling heaven
by superstition,
drunk and happy
on a chapel gable.

I would roost a night
on the slab of exile,
then hide in the cleft
of that churchyard wall

where hand after hand
keeps wearing away
at the cold, hard-breasted
votive granite.

And follow me.
I would migrate
through a high cave mouth
into an oaten, sun-warmed cliff,

on down the soft-nubbed,

clay-floored passage,
face-brush, wing-flap,
to the deepest chamber.

There a drinking deer
is cut into rock,
its haunch and neck
rise with the contours,

the incised outline
curves to a strained
expectant muzzle
and a nostril flared

at a dried-up source.
For my book of changes
I would meditate
that stone-faced vigil

until the long dumbfounded
spirit broke cover
to raise a dust
in the font of exhaustion.

Notes

'Away from it all': '*I was stretched...*' from Czeslaw Milosz's *Native Realm*(University of California Press, 1981), p. 125.

'Chekhov on Sakhalin': Chekhov's friends presented him with a bottle of cognac on the eve of his departure for the prison island of Sakhalin, where he spent the summer of 1890 interviewing all the criminals and political prisoners. His book on conditions in the penal colony was published in 1895.

'Sandstone Keepsake': Guy de Montfort. See *Inferno*, Canto XII, lines 118–20, and also Dorothy Sayers's note in her translation (Penguin Classics).

'The King of the Ditchbacks': see note on Part Three.

PART TWO: STATION ISLAND

Station Island is a sequence of dream encounters with familiar ghosts, set on Station Island on Lough Derg in Co. Donegal. The island is also known as St Patrick's Purgatory because of a tradition that Patrick was the first to establish the penitential vigil of fasting and praying which still constitutes the basis of the three-day pilgrimage. Each unit of the contemporary pilgrim's exercises is called a 'station', and a large part of each station involves walking barefoot and praying round the 'beds', stone circles which are said to be the remains of early medieval monastic cells.

Section II: William Carleton (1794–1869), a Catholic by birth, had done the pilgrimage in his youth, and when he converted to the Established Church he published his critical account of it in 'The Lough Derg Pilgrim' and launched himself upon his most famous work, *Traits and Stories of the Irish Peasantry* (1830–3).

Section V: 'Forty-two years on...' Patrick Kavanagh wrote his posthumously published poem, 'Lough Derg', in 1942.

Section VI: 'Till Phoebus...', Horace, Odes, Book III, xxi, line 24. 'As little flowers...', Dante, *Inferno*, Canto II, lines 127–32.

Section XI: The St John of the Cross poem translated here is 'Cantar del alma que se huelga de conoscer a Dios por fe'.

Section XII: 'Stephen's diary'. See the end of James Joyce's *Portrait of the Artist as a Young Man*.

PART THREE: SWEENEY REDIVIVUS

The poems in this section are voiced for Sweeney, the seventh-century Ulster king who was transformed into a bird-man and exiled to the trees by the curse of St Ronan. A version of the Irish tale is available in my *Sweeney Astray*, but I trust these glosses can survive without the support system of the original story. Many of them, of course, are imagined in contexts far removed from early medieval Ireland.

S.H.
February 1984

The Haw Lantern

For Bernard and Jane McCabe

The riverbed, dried-up, half-full of leaves.
Us, listening to a river in the trees.

Contents

345   Alphabets

348   Terminus

350   From the Frontier of Writing

351   The Haw Lantern

352   The Stone Grinder

353   A Daylight Art

354   Parable Island

356   From the Republic of Conscience

358   Hailstones

360   Two Quick Notes

361   The Stone Verdict

362   From the Land of the Unspoken

363   A Ship of Death

364   The Spoonbait

365   In Memoriam: Robert Fitzgerald

366   The Old Team

367   Clearances

376   The Milk Factory

377   The Summer of Lost Rachel

379   The Wishing Tree

380   A Postcard from Iceland

381   A Peacock's Feather

383 Grotus and Coventina

384 Holding Course

385 The Song of the Bullets

387 Wolfe Tone

388 A Shooting Script

389 From the Canton of Expectation

391 The Mud Vision

393 The Disappearing Island

394 The Riddle

Acknowledgements

Acknowledgements are due to the editors of the following magazines where some of these poems appeared for the first time: *Field, Gown, Harper's, Harvard Magazine, Honest Ulsterman, Ireland of the Welcomes, Irish Times, London Review of Books, Numbers, Ploughshares, Poetry Book Society Supplement, Poetry Ireland Review, The Scotsman Seneca Review, Threepenny Review, Times Literary Supplement, Verse.*

Nine of the poems appeared in *Hailstones* (Gallery Press, 1984).

An earlier version of the sequence 'Clearances' was published in a limited edition by Cornamona Press in 1986.

"From the Republic of Conscience' was published as a pamphlet by Amnesty International, Irish Section, on Human Rights Day, 1985.

'Alphabets' was the Phi Beta Kappa poem at Harvard University in 1984.

'Parable Island' was written for William Golding and included in *William Golding, The Man and his Books: A Tribute on his 75th Birthday* (Faber and Faber, 1986); 'The Disappearing Island' was first read at a dinner for Tim Severin organized by the St Brendan Society.

Alphabets

I

A shadow his father makes with joined hands
And thumbs and fingers nibbles on the wall
Like a rabbit's head. He understands
He will understand more when he goes to school.

There he draws smoke with chalk the whole first week,
Then draws the forked stick that they call a Y.
This is writing. A swan's neck and swan's back
Make the 2 he can see now as well as say.

Two rafters and a cross-tie on the slate
Are the letter some call *ah*, some call *ay*.
There are charts, there are headlines, there is a right
Way to hold the pen and a wrong way.

First it is 'copying out', and then 'English'
Marked correct with a little leaning hoe.
Smells of inkwells rise in the classroom hush.
A globe in the window tilts like a coloured O.

II

Declensions sang on air like a *hosanna*
As, column after stratified column,
Book One of *Elementa Latina*,
Marbled and minatory, rose up in him.

For he was fostered next in a stricter school
Named for the patron saint of the oak wood
Where classes switched to the pealing of a bell
And he left the Latin forum for the shade

Of new calligraphy that felt like home.

The letters of this alphabet were trees.
The capitals were orchards in full bloom,
The lines of script like briars coiled in ditches.

Here in her snooded garment and bare feet,
All ringleted in assonance and woodnotes,
The poet's dream stole over him like sunlight
And passed into the tenebrous thickets.

He learns this other writing. He is the scribe
Who drove a team of quills on his white field.
Round his cell door the blackbirds dart and dab.
Then self-denial, fasting, the pure cold.

By rules that hardened the farther they reached north
He bends to his desk and begins again.
Christ's sickle has been in the undergrowth.
The script grows bare and Merovingian.

III

The globe has spun. He stands in a wooden O.
He alludes to Shakespeare. He alludes to Graves.
Time has bulldozed the school and school window.
Balers drop bales like printouts where stooked sheaves

Made lambdas on the stubble once at harvest
And the delta face of each potato pit
Was patted straight and moulded against frost.
All gone, with the omega that kept

Watch above each door, the good luck horse-shoe.
Yet shape-note language, absolute on air
As Constantine's sky-lettered IN HOC SIGNO
Can still command him; or the necromancer

Who would hang from the domed ceiling of his house
A figure of the world with colours in it

So that the figure of the universe
And 'not just single things' would meet his sight

When he walked abroad. As from his small window
The astronaut sees all he has sprung from,
The risen, aqueous, singular, lucent O
Like a magnified and buoyant ovum –

Or like my own wide pre-reflective stare
All agog at the plasterer on his ladder
Skimming our gable and writing our name there
With his trowel point, letter by strange letter.

Terminus

I

When I hoked there, I would find
An acorn and a rusted bolt.

If I lifted my eyes, a factory chimney
And a dormant mountain.

If I listened, an engine shunting
And a trotting horse.

Is it any wonder when I thought
I would have second thoughts?

II

When they spoke of the prudent squirrel's hoard
It shone like gifts at a nativity.

When they spoke of the mammon of iniquity
The coins in my pockets reddened like stove-lids.

I was the march drain and the march drain's banks
Suffering the limit of each claim.

III

Two buckets were easier carried than one.
I grew up in between.

My left hand placed the standard iron weight.
My right tilted a last grain in the balance.

Baronies, parishes met where I was born.
When I stood on the central stepping stone

I was the last earl on horseback in midstream
Still parleying, in earshot of his peers.

From the Frontier of Writing

The tightness and the nilness round that space
when the car stops in the road, the troops inspect
its make and number and, as one bends his face

towards your window, you catch sight of more
on a hill beyond, eyeing with intent
down cradled guns that hold you under cover

and everything is pure interrogation
until a rifle motions and you move
with guarded unconcerned acceleration –

a little emptier, a little spent
as always by that quiver in the self,
subjugated, yes, and obedient.

So you drive on to the frontier of writing
where it happens again. The guns on tripods;
the sergeant with his on-off mike repeating

data about you, waiting for the squawk
of clearance; the marksman training down
out of the sun upon you like a hawk.

And suddenly you're through, arraigned yet freed,
as if you'd passed from behind a waterfall
on the black current of a tarmac road

past armour-plated vehicles, out between
the posted soldiers flowing and receding
like tree shadows into the polished windscreen.

The Haw Lantern

The wintry haw is burning out of season,
crab of the thorn, a small light for small people,
wanting no more from them but that they keep
the wick of self-respect from dying out,
not having to blind them with illumination.

But sometimes when your breath plumes in the frost
it takes the roaming shape of Diogenes
with his lantern, seeking one just man;
so you end up scrutinized from behind the haw
he holds up at eye-level on its twig,
and you flinch before its bonded pith and stone,
its blood-prick that you wish would test and clear you,
its pecked-at ripeness that scans you, then moves on.

The Stone Grinder

Penelope worked with some guarantee of a plot.
Whatever she unweaved at night
might advance it all by a day.

Me, I ground the same stones for fifty years
and what I undid was never the thing I had done.
I was unrewarded as darkness at a mirror.

I prepared my surface to survive what came over it —
cartographers, printmakers, all that lining and inking.
I ordained opacities and they haruspicated.

For them it was a new start and a clean slate
every time. For me, it was coming full circle
like the ripple perfected in stillness.

So. To commemorate me. Imagine the faces
stripped off the face of a quarry. Practise
coitus interruptus on a pile of old lithographs.

A Daylight Art

for Norman MacCaig

On the day he was to take the poison
Socrates told his friends he had been writing:
putting Aesop's fables into verse.

And this was not because Socrates loved wisdom
and advocated the examined life.
The reason was that he had had a dream.

Caesar, now, or Herod or Constantine
or any number of Shakespearean kings
bursting at the end like dams

where original panoramas lie submerged
which have to rise again before the death scenes –
you can believe in their believing dreams.

But hardly Socrates. Until, that is,
he tells his friends the dream had kept recurring
all his life, repeating one instruction:

Practise the art, which art until that moment
he always took to mean philosophy.
Happy the man, therefore, with a natural gift

for practising the right one from the start –
poetry, say, or fishing; whose nights are dreamless;
whose deep-sunk panoramas rise and pass

like daylight through the rod's eye or the nib's eye.

Parable Island

Although they are an occupied nation
and their only border is an inland one
they yield to nobody in their belief
that the country is an island.

Somewhere in the far north, in a region
every native thinks of as 'the coast',
there lies the mountain of the shifting names.

The occupiers call it Cape Basalt.
The Sun's Headstone, say farmers in the east.
Drunken westerners call it The Orphan's Tit.

To find out where he stands the traveller
has to keep listening – since there is no map
which draws the line he knows he must have crossed.

Meanwhile, the forked-tongued natives keep repeating
prophecies they pretend not to believe
about a point where all the names converge
underneath the mountain and where (some day)
they are going to start to mine the ore of truth.

II

In the beginning there was one bell-tower
which struck its single note each day at noon
in honour of the one-eyed all-creator.

At least, this was the original idea
missionary scribes record they found
in autochthonous tradition. But even there

you can't be sure that parable is not
at work already retrospectively,
since all their early manuscripts are full

of stylized eye-shapes and recurrent glosses
in which those old revisionists derive
the word *island* from roots in *eye* and *land*.

III

Now archaeologists begin to gloss the glosses.
To one school, the stone circles are pure symbol;
to another, assembly spots or hut foundations.

One school thinks a post-hole in an ancient floor
stands first of all for a pupil in an iris.
The other thinks a post-hole is a post-hole. And so on –

like the subversives and collaborators
always vying with a fierce possessiveness
for the right to set 'the island story' straight.

IV

The elders dream of boat-journeys and havens
and have their stories too, like the one about the man
who took to his bed, it seems, and died convinced

that the cutting of the Panama Canal
would mean the ocean would all drain away
and the island disappear by aggrandizement.

From the Republic of Conscience

I

When I landed in the republic of conscience
it was so noiseless when the engines stopped
I could hear a curlew high above the runway.

At immigration, the clerk was an old man
who produced a wallet from his homespun coat
and showed me a photograph of my grandfather.

The woman in customs asked me to declare
the words of our traditional cures and charms
to heal dumbness and avert the evil eye.

No porters. No interpreter. No taxi.
You carried your own burden and very soon
your symptoms of creeping privilege disappeared.

II

Fog is a dreaded omen there but lightning
spells universal good and parents hang
swaddled infants in trees during thunderstorms.

Salt is their precious mineral. And seashells
are held to the ear during births and funerals.
The base of all inks and pigments is seawater.

Their sacred symbol is a stylized boat.
The sail is an ear, the mast a sloping pen,
The hull a mouth-shape, the keel an open eye.

At their inauguration, public leaders
must swear to uphold unwritten law and weep
to atone for their presumption to hold office –

and to affirm their faith that all life sprang
from salt in tears which the sky-god wept
after he dreamt his solitude was endless.

III

I came back from that frugal republic
with my two arms the one length, the customs woman
having insisted my allowance was myself.

The old man rose and gazed into my face
and said that was official recognition
that I was now a dual citizen.

He therefore desired me when I got home
to consider myself a representative
and to speak on their behalf in my own tongue.

Their embassies, he said, were everywhere
but operated independently
and no ambassador would ever be relieved.

Hailstones

I

My cheek was hit and hit:
sudden hailstones
pelted and bounced on the road.

When it cleared again
something whipped and knowledgeable
had withdrawn

and left me there with my chances.
I made a small hard ball
of burning water running from my hand

just as I make this now
out of the melt of the real thing
smarting into its absence.

II

To be reckoned with, all the same,
those brats of showers.
The way they refused permission,

rattling the classroom window
like a ruler across the knuckles,
the way they were perfect first

and then in no time dirty slush.
Thomas Traherne had his orient wheat
for proof and wonder

but for us, it was the sting of hailstones
and the unstingable hands of Eddie Diamond
foraging in the nettles.

III

Nipple and hive, bite-lumps,
small acorns of the almost pleasurable
intimated and disallowed

when the shower ended
and everything said *wait*.
For what? For forty years

to say there, there you had
the truest foretaste of your aftermath –
in that dilation

when the light opened in silence
and a car with wipers going still
laid perfect tracks in the slush.

Two Quick Notes

I

My old hard friend, how you sought
Occasions of justified anger!
Who could buff me like you

Who wanted the soul to ring true
And plain as a galvanized bucket
And would kick it to test it?

Or whack it clean like a carpet.
So of course when you turned on yourself
You were ferocious.

II

Abrupt and thornproofed and lonely.
A raider from the old country
Of night prayer and principled challenge,

Crashing at barriers
You thought ought still to be there,
Overshooting into thin air.

O upright self-wounding prie-dieu
In shattered free fall:
Hail and farewell.

The Stone Verdict

When he stands in the judgment place
With his stick in his hand and the broad hat
Still on his head, maimed by self-doubt
And an old disdain of sweet talk and excuses,
It will be no justice if the sentence is blabbed out.
He will expect more than words in the ultimate court
He relied on through a lifetime's speechlessness.

Let it be like the judgment of Hermes,
God of the stone heap, where the stones were
verdicts
Cast solidly at his feet, piling up around him
Until he stood waist deep in the cairn
Of his apotheosis: maybe a gate-pillar
Or a tumbled wallstead where hogweed earths the
    silence
Somebody will break at last to say, 'Here
His spirit lingers,' and will have said too much.

From the Land of the Unspoken

I have heard of a bar of platinum
kept by a logical and talkative nation
as their standard of measurement,
the throne room and the burial chamber
of every calculation and prediction.
I could feel at home inside that metal core
slumbering at the very hub of systems.

We are a dispersed people whose history
is a sensation of opaque fidelity.
When or why our exile began
among the speech-ridden, we cannot tell
but solidarity comes flooding up in us
when we hear their legends of infants discovered
floating in coracles towards destiny
or of kings' biers heaved and borne away
on the river's shoulders or out into the sea roads.

When we recognize our own, we fall in step
but do not altogether come up level.
My deepest contact was underground
strap-hanging back to back on a rush-hour train
and in a museum once, I inhaled
vernal assent from a neck and shoulder
pretending to be absorbed in a display
of absolutely silent quernstones.

Our unspoken assumptions have the force
of revelation. How else could we know
that whoever is the first of us to seek
assent and votes in a rich democracy
will be the last of us and have killed our language?
Meanwhile, if we miss the sight of a fish
we heard jumping and then see its ripples,
that means one more of us is dying somewhere.

A Ship of Death

Scyld was still a strong man when his time came
and he crossed over into Our Lord's keeping.
His warrior band did what he bade them
when he laid down the law among the Danes:
they shouldered him out to the sea's flood,
the chief they revered who had long ruled them.
A ring-necked prow rode in the harbour,
clad with ice, its cables tightening.
They stretched their beloved lord in the boat,
laid out amidships by the mast
the great ring-giver. Far-fetched treasures
were piled upon him, and precious gear.
I never heard before of a ship so well furbished
with battle-tackle, bladed weapons
and coats of mail. The treasure was massed
on top of him: it would travel far
on out into the sway of ocean.
They decked his body no less bountifully
with offerings than those first ones did
who cast him away when he was a child
and launched him out alone over the waves.
And they set a gold standard up
high above his head and let him drift
to wind and tide, bewailing him
and mourning their loss. No man can tell,
no wise man in the hall or weathered veteran
knows for certain who salvaged that load.

Beowulf, ll., 26–52

The Spoonbait

So a new similitude is given us
And we say: The soul may be compared

Unto a spoonbait that a child discovers
Beneath the sliding lid of a pencil case,

Glimpsed once and imagined for a lifetime
Risen and free and spooling out of nowhere –

A shooting star going back up the darkness.
It flees him and it burns him all at once

Like the single drop that Dives implored
Falling and falling into a great gulf.

Then exit, the polished helmet of a hero
Laid out amidships above scudding water.

Exit, alternatively, a toy of light
Reeled through him upstream, snagging on nothing.

In Memoriam: Robert Fitzgerald

The socket of each axehead like the squared
Doorway to a megalithic tomb
With its slabbed passage that keeps opening forward
To face another corbelled stone-faced door
That opens on a third. There is no last door,
Just threshold stone, stone jambs, stone crossbeam
Repeating *enter, enter, enter, enter*.
Lintel and upright fly past in the dark.

After the bowstring sang a swallow's note,
The arrow whose migration is its mark
Leaves a whispered breath in every socket.
The great test over, while the gut's still humming,
This time it travels out of all knowing
Perfectly aimed towards the vacant centre.

The Old Team

Dusk. Scope of air. A railed pavilion
Formal and blurring in the sepia
Of (always) summery Edwardian
Ulster. Which could be India
Or England. Or any old parade ground
Where a moustachioed tenantry togged out
To pose with folded arms, all musclebound
And staunch and forever up against it.

Moyola Park FC! Sons of Castledawson!
Stokers and scutchers! Grandfather McCann!
Team spirit, walled parkland, the linen mill
Have, in your absence, grown historical
As those lightly clapped, dull-thumping games of football.
The steady coffins sail past at eye-level.

Clearances

in memoriam M.K.H., 1911–1984

She taught me what her uncle once taught her:
How easily the biggest coal block split
If you got the grain and hammer angled right.

The sound of that relaxed alluring blow,
Its co-opted and obliterated echo,
Taught me to hit, taught me to loosen,

Taught me between the hammer and the block
To face the music. Teach me now to listen,
To strike it rich behind the linear black.

1

A cobble thrown a hundred years ago
Keeps coming at me, the first stone
Aimed at a great-grandmother's turncoat brow.
The pony jerks and the riot's on.
She's crouched low in the trap
Running the gauntlet that first Sunday
Down the brae to Mass at a panicked gallop.
He whips on through the town to cries of 'Lundy!'

Call her 'The Convert'. 'The Exogamous Bride'.
Anyhow, it is a genre piece
Inherited on my mother's side
And mine to dispose with now she's gone.
Instead of silver and Victorian lace,
The exonerating, exonerated stone.

2

Polished linoleum shone there. Brass taps shone.
The china cups were very white and big –
An unchipped set with sugar bowl and jug.
The kettle whistled. Sandwich and teascone
Were present and correct. In case it run,
The butter must be kept out of the sun.
And don't be dropping crumbs. Don't tilt your chair
Don't reach. Don't point. Don't make noise when you stir.

It is Number 5, New Row, Land of the Dead,
Where grandfather is rising from his place
With spectacles pushed back on a clean bald head
To welcome a bewildered homing daughter
Before she even knocks. 'What's this? What's this?'
And they sit down in the shining room together.

When all the others were away at Mass
I was all hers as we peeled potatoes.
They broke the silence, let fall one by one
Like solder weeping off the soldering iron:
Cold comforts set between us, things to share
Gleaming in a bucket of clean water.
And again let fall. Little pleasant splashes
From each other's work would bring us to our senses.

So while the parish priest at her bedside
Went hammer and tongs at the prayers for the dying
And some were responding and some crying
I remembered her head bent towards my head,
Her breath in mine, our fluent dipping knives –
Never closer the whole rest of our lives.

4

Fear of affectation made her affect
Inadequacy whenever it came to
Pronouncing words 'beyond her'. *Bertold Brek.*
She'd manage something hampered and askew
Every time, as if she might betray
The hampered and inadequate by too
Well-adjusted a vocabulary.
With more challenge than pride, she'd tell me, 'You
Know all them things.' So I governed my tongue
In front of her, a genuinely well-
adjusted adequate betrayal
Of what I knew better. I'd *naw* and *aye*
And decently relapse into the wrong
Grammar which kept us allied and at bay.

The cool that came off sheets just off the line
Made me think the damp must still be in them
But when I took my corners of the linen
And pulled against her, first straight down the hem
And then diagonally, then flapped and shook
The fabric like a sail in a cross-wind,
They made a dried-out undulating thwack.
So we'd stretch and fold and end up hand to hand
For a split second as if nothing had happened
For nothing had that had not always happened
Beforehand, day by day, just touch and go,
Coming close again by holding back
In moves where I was x and she was o
Inscribed in sheets she'd sewn from ripped-out flour sacks.

In the first flush of the Easter holidays
The ceremonies during Holy Week
Were highpoints of our *Sons and Lovers* phase.
The midnight fire. The paschal candlestick.
Elbow to elbow, glad to be kneeling next
To each other up there near the front
Of the packed church, we would follow the text
And rubrics for the blessing of the font.
As the hind longs for the streams, so my soul...
Dippings. Towellings. The water breathed on.
The water mixed with chrism and with oil.
Cruet tinkle. Formal incensation
And the psalmist's outcry taken up with pride:
Day and night my tears have been my bread.

In the last minutes he said more to her
Almost than in all their life together.
'You'll be in New Row on Monday night
And I'll come up for you and you'll be glad
When I walk in the door... Isn't that right?'
His head was bent down to her propped-up head.
She could not hear but we were overjoyed.
He called her good and girl. Then she was dead,
The searching for a pulsebeat was abandoned
And we all knew one thing by being there.
The space we stood around had been emptied
Into us to keep, it penetrated
Clearances that suddenly stood open.
High cries were felled and a pure change happened.

I thought of walking round and round a space
Utterly empty, utterly a source
Where the decked chestnut tree had lost its place
In our front hedge above the wallflowers.
The white chips jumped and jumped and skited high.
I heard the hatchet's differentiated
Accurate cut, the crack, the sigh
And collapse of what luxuriated
Through the shocked tips and wreckage of it all.
Deep planted and long gone, my coeval
Chestnut from a jam jar in a hole,
Its heft and hush become a bright nowhere,
A soul ramifying and forever
Silent, beyond silence listened for.

The Milk Factory

Scuts of froth swirled from the discharge pipe.
We halted on the other bank and watched
A milky water run from the pierced side
Of milk itself, the crock of its substance spilt
Across white limbo floors where shift-workers
Waded round the clock, and the factory
Kept its distance like a bright-decked star-ship.

There we go, soft-eyed calves of the dew,
Astonished and assumed into fluorescence.

The Summer of Lost Rachel

Potato crops are flowering,
    Hard green plums appear
On damson trees at your back door
    And every berried briar

Is glittering and dripping
    Whenever showers plout down
On flooded hay and flooding drills.
    There's a ring around the moon.

The whole summer was waterlogged
    Yet everyone is loath
To trust the rain's soft-soaping ways
    And sentiments of growth

Because all confidence in summer's
    Unstinting largesse
Broke down last May when we laid you out
    In white, your whited face

Gashed from the accident, but still,
    So absolutely still,
And the setting sun set merciless
    And every merciful

Register inside us yearned
    To run the film back,
For you to step into the road
    Wheeling your bright-rimmed bike,

Safe and sound as usual,
    Across, then down the lane,
The twisted spokes all straightened out,
    The awful skid-marks gone.

But no. So let the downpours flood
    Our memory's riverbed
Until, in thick-webbed currents,
    The life you might have led

Wavers and tugs dreamily
    As soft-plumed waterweed
Which tempts our gaze and quietens it
    And recollects our need.

The Wishing Tree

I thought of her as the wishing tree that died
And saw it lifted, root and branch, to heaven,
Trailing a shower of all that had been driven

Need by need by need into its hale
Sap-wood and bark: coin and pin and nail
Came streaming from it like a comet-tail

New-minted and dissolved. I had a vision
Of an airy branch-head rising through damp cloud,
Of turned-up faces where the tree had stood.

A Postcard from Iceland

As I dipped to test the stream some yards away
From a hot spring, I could hear nothing
But the whole mud-slick muttering and boiling.

And then my guide behind me saying,
'Lukewarm. And I think you'd want to know
That *luk* was an old Icelandic word for hand.'

And you would want to know (but you know already)
How usual that waft and pressure felt
When the inner palm of water found my palm.

A Peacock's Feather

for Daisy Garnett

Six days ago the water fell
To christen you, to work its spell
And wipe your slate, we hope, for good.
But now your life is sleep and food
Which, with the touch of love, suffice
You, Daisy, Daisy, English niece.

Gloucestershire: its prospects lie
Wooded and misty to my eye
Whose landscape, as your mother's was,
Is other than this mellowness
Of topiary, lawn and brick,
Possessed, untrespassed, walled, nostalgic.

I come from scraggy farm and moss,
Old patchworks that the pitch and toss
Of history have left dishevelled.
But here, for your sake, I have levelled
My cart-track voice to garden tones,
Cobbled the bog with Cotswold stones.

Ravelling strands of families mesh
In love-knots of two minds, one flesh.
The future's not our own. We'll weave
An in-law maze, we'll nod and wave
With trust but little intimacy –
So this is a billet-doux to say

That in a warm July you lay
Christened and smiling in Bradley
While I, a guest in your green court,
At a west window sat and wrote
Self-consciously in gathering dark.

I might as well be in Coole Park.

So before I leave your ordered home,
Let us pray. May tilth and loam,
Darkened with Celts' and Saxons' blood,
Breastfeed your love of house and wood –
Where I drop this for you, as I pass,
Like the peacock's feather on the grass.

1972

Grotus and Coventina

Far from home Grotus dedicated an altar to Coventina
Who holds in her right hand a waterweed
And in her left a pitcher spilling out a river.
Anywhere Grotus looked at running water he felt at home
And when he remembered the stone where he cut his name
Some dried-up course beneath his breastbone started
Pouring and darkening – more or less the way
The thought of his stunted altar works on me.

Remember when our electric pump gave out,
Priming it with bucketfuls, our idiotic rage
And hangdog phone-calls to the farm next door
For somebody please to come and fix it?
And when it began to hammer on again,
Jubilation at the tap's full force, the sheer
Given fact of water, how you felt you'd never
Waste one drop but know its worth better always.
Do you think we could run through all that one more time?
I'll be Grotus, you be Coventina.

Holding Course

Propellers underwater, cabins drumming, lights –
Unthought-of but constant out there every night,
The big ferries pondered on their courses.
I envy you your sight of them this morning,
Docked and massive with their sloped-back funnels.

The outlook is high and airy where you stand
By our attic window. Far Toledo blues.
And from a shelf behind you
The alpine thistle we brought from Covadonga
Inclines its jaggy crest.

Last autumn we were smouldering and parched
As those spikes that keep vigil overhead
Like Grendel's steely talon nailed
To the mead-hall roof. And then we broke through
Or we came through. It was its own reward.

We are voluptuaries of the morning after.
As gulls cry out above the deep channels
And you stand on and on, twiddling your hair,
Think of me as your MacWhirr of the boudoir,
Head on, one track, ignorant of manoeuvre.

The Song of the Bullets

I watched a long time in the yard
    The usual stars, the still
And seemly planets, lantern-bright
    Above our darkened hill.

And then a star that moved, I thought,
    For something moved indeed
Up from behind the massed skyline
    At ardent silent speed

And when it reached the zenith, cut
    Across the curving path
Of a second light that swung up like
    A scythe-point through its swathe.

'The sky at night is full of us',
    Now one began to sing,
'Our slugs of lead lie cold and dead,
    Our trace is on the wing.

Our casings and our blunted parts
    Are gathered up below
As justice stands aghast and stares
    Like the sun on arctic snow.

Our guilt was accidental. Blame,
    Blame because you must.
Then blame young men for semen or
    Blame the moon for moondust.'

As ricochets that warble close,
    Then die away on wind,
That hard contralto sailed across
    And stellar quiet reigned

Until the other fireball spoke:
    'We are the iron will.
We hoop and cooper worlds beyond
    The killer and the kill.

Mount Olivet's beatitudes,
    The soul's cadenced desires
Cannot prevail against us who
    Dwell in the marbled fires

Of every steady eye that ever
    Narrowed, sighted, paused:
We fire and glaze the shape of things
    Until the shape's imposed.'

Now wind was blowing through the yard.
    Clouds blanked the stars. The still
And seemly planets disappeared
    Above our darkened hill.

Wolfe Tone

Light as a skiff, manoeuvrable
yet outmanoeuvred,

I affected epaulettes and a cockade,
wrote a style well-bred and impervious

to the solidarity I angled for,
and played the ancient Roman with a razor.

I was the shouldered oar that ended up
far from the brine and whiff of venture,

like a scratching-post or a crossroads flagpole,
out of my element among small farmers –

I who once wakened to the shouts of men
rising from the bottom of the sea,

men in their shirts mounting through deep water
when the Atlantic stove our cabin's dead lights in

and the big fleet split and Ireland dwindled
as we ran before the gale under bare poles.

A Shooting Script

They are riding away from whatever might have been
Towards what will never be, in a held shot:
Teachers on bicycles, saluting native speakers,
Treading the nineteen-twenties like the future.

Still pedalling out at the end of the lens,
Not getting anywhere and not getting away.
Mix to fuchsia that 'follows the language'.
A long soundless sequence. Pan and fade.

Then voices over, in different Irishes,
Discussing translation jobs and rates per line;
Like nineteenth-century milestones in grass verges,
Occurrence of names like R. M. Ballantyne.

A close-up on the cat's eye of a button
Pulling back wide to the cape of a soutane,
Biretta, Roman collar, Adam's apple.
Freeze his blank face. Let the credits run

And just when it looks as if it is all over –
Tracking shots of a long wave up a strand
That breaks towards the point of a stick writing and writing
Words in the old script in the running sand.

From the Canton of Expectation

I

We lived deep in a land of optative moods,
under high, banked clouds of resignation.
A rustle of loss in the phrase *Not in our lifetime*,
the broken nerve when we prayed *Vouchsafe* or *Deign*,
were creditable, sufficient to the day.

Once a year we gathered in a field
of dance platforms and tents where children sang
songs they had learned by rote in the old language.
An auctioneer who had fought in the brotherhood
enumerated the humiliations
we always took for granted, but not even he
considered this, I think, a call to action.
Iron-mouthed loudspeakers shook the air
yet nobody felt blamed. He had confirmed us.
When our rebel anthem played the meeting shut
we turned for home and the usual harassment
by militiamen on overtime at roadblocks.

II

And next thing, suddenly, this change of mood.
Books open in the newly-wired kitchens.
Young heads that might have dozed a life away
against the flanks of milking cows were busy
paving and pencilling their first causeways
across the prescribed texts. The paving stones
of quadrangles came next and a grammar
of imperatives, the new age of demands.
They would banish the conditional for ever,
this generation born impervious to
the triumph in our cries of *de profundis*.
Our faith in winning by enduring most

they made anathema, intelligences
brightened and unmannerly as crowbars.

III

What looks the strongest has outlived its term.
The future lies with what's affirmed from under.
These things that corroborated us when we dwelt
under the aegis of our stealthy patron,
the guardian angel of passivity,
now sink a fang of menace in my shoulder.
I repeat the word 'stricken' to myself
and stand bareheaded under the banked clouds
edged more and more with brassy thunderlight.
I yearn for hammerblows on clinkered planks,
the uncompromised report of driven thole-pins,
to know there is one among us who never swerved
from all his instincts told him was right action,
who stood his ground in the indicative,
whose boat will lift when the cloudburst happens.

The Mud Vision

Statues with exposed hearts and barbed-wire crowns
Still stood in alcoves, hares flitted beneath
The dozing bellies of jets, our menu-writers
And punks with aerosol sprays held their own
With the best of them. Satellite link-ups
Wafted over us the blessings of popes, heliports
Maintained a charmed circle for idols on tour
And casualties on their stretchers. We sleepwalked
The line between panic and formulae, screentested
Our first native models and the last of the mummers,
Watching ourselves at a distance, advantaged
And airy as a man on a springboard
Who keeps limbering up because the man cannot dive.

And then in the foggy midlands it appeared,
Our mud vision, as if a rose window of mud
Had invented itself out of the glittery damp,
A gossamer wheel, concentric with its own hub
Of nebulous dirt, sullied yet lucent.
We had heard of the sun standing still and the sun
That changed colour, but we were vouchsafed
Original clay, transfigured and spinning.
And then the sunsets ran murky, the wiper
Could never entirely clean off the windscreen,
Reservoirs tasted of silt, a light fuzz
Accrued in the hair and the eyebrows, and some
Took to wearing a smudge on their foreheads
To be prepared for whatever. Vigils
Began to be kept around puddled gaps,
On altars bulrushes ousted the lilies
And a rota of invalids came and went
On beds they could lease placed in range of the shower.

A generation who had seen a sign!

Those nights when we stood in an umber dew and smelled
Mould in the verbena, or woke to a light
Furrow-breath on the pillow, when the talk
Was all about who had seen it and our fear
Was touched with a secret pride, only ourselves
Could be adequate then to our lives. When the rainbow
Curved flood-brown and ran like a water-rat's back
So that drivers on the hard shoulder switched off to watch,
We wished it away, and yet we presumed it a test
That would prove us beyond expectation.

We lived, of course, to learn the folly of that.
One day it was gone and the east gable
Where its trembling corolla had balanced
Was starkly a ruin again, with dandelions
Blowing high up on the ledges, and moss
That slumbered on through its increase. As cameras raked
The site from every angle, experts
Began their *post factum* jabber and all of us
Crowded in tight for the big explanations.
Just like that, we forgot that the vision was ours,
Our one chance to know the incomparable
And dive to a future. What might have been origin
We dissipated in news. The clarified place
Had retrieved neither us nor itself – except
You could say we survived. So say that, and watch us
Who had our chance to be mud-men, convinced and
    estranged,
Figure in our own eyes for the eyes of the world.

The Disappearing Island

Once we presumed to found ourselves for good
Between its blue hills and those sandless shores
Where we spent our desperate night in prayer and vigil,

Once we had gathered driftwood, made a hearth
And hung our cauldron like a firmament,
The island broke beneath us like a wave.

The land sustaining us seemed to hold firm
Only when we embraced it *in extremis.*
All I believe that happened there was vision.

The Riddle

You never saw it used but still can hear
The sift and fall of stuff hopped on the mesh,

Clods and buds in a little dust-up,
The dribbled pile accruing under it.

Which would be better, what sticks or what falls through?
Or does the choice itself create the value?

Legs apart, deft-handed, start a mime
To sift the sense of things from what's imagined

And work out what was happening in that story
Of the man who carried water in a riddle.

Was it culpable ignorance, or was it rather
A *via negativa* through drops and let-downs?

Station Island by SEAMUS HEANEY

First published in 1984

The Haw Lantern by SEAMUS HEANEY

First published in 1987

This edition arranged with Faber and Faber Ltd. through Big Apple Agency, Inc., Labuan, Malaysia

Simplified Chinese edition copyright © 2024 Guangxi Normal University Press Group Co., Ltd.

著作权合同登记号桂图登字:20 - 2024 - 003 号

图书在版编目(CIP)数据

斯泰森岛;山楂灯笼:汉、英/(爱尔兰)谢默斯·希尼著;朱玉译. —桂林:广西师范大学出版社,2024.5

(文学纪念碑)

书名原文:Station Island/The Haw Lantern

ISBN 978 - 7 - 5598 - 6904 - 3

Ⅰ. ①斯… Ⅱ. ①谢… ②朱… Ⅲ. ①诗集-爱尔兰-现代-汉、英 Ⅳ. ①I562.25

中国国家版本馆 CIP 数据核字(2024)第 081961 号

斯泰森岛·山楂灯笼:汉、英

SITAISEN DAO · SHANZHA DENGLONG:HAN、YING

出 品 人:刘广汉　　策　　划:魏　东　　责任编辑:魏　东　程卫平
助理编辑:钟雨晴　　装帧设计:赵　瑾

广西师范大学出版社出版发行

(广西桂林市五里店路9号　　邮政编码:541004)
(网址:http://www.bbtpress.com)

出版人:黄轩庄

全国新华书店经销

销售热线:021 - 65200318　021 - 31260822 - 898

山东临沂新华印刷物流集团有限责任公司印刷

(临沂高新技术产业开发区新华路1号　邮政编码:276017)

开本:889 mm×1 194 mm　　1/32

印张:12.5　　　　　　　　字数:367 千

2024 年 5 月第 1 版　　2024 年 5 月第 1 次印刷

定价:78.00 元